Addiction and Faith

Winning the Battle Against Addictive
Behaviors with God's Help

Reverend Michael K. Mason

RIVER BIRCH PRESS

Mesa, Arizona

Scripture quotations marked NIV are taken from THE HOLY BIBLE: New International Version ©1978 by the New York International Bible Society, used by permission of Zondervan Bible Publishers.

ISBN 978-1-956365-56-6 (print)
ISBN 978-1-956365-57-3 (e-book)

For Worldwide Distribution
Printed in the U.S.A.

River Birch Press
P.O. Box 7341, Mesa, AZ 85216

Contents

PHASE IV: Learning to Accept God's Love and Live an Addiction-Free Life *91*

iv

Preface

So if the Son sets you free, you will be free indeed (John 8:36).

Trying to solve the riddle of addiction can be as challenging as attempting to complete a jigsaw puzzle without the benefit of the picture on the box. Many misshapen pieces are almost impossible to fit together without a broader view of the topic.

While addiction is undoubtedly a complicated issue, it has never been more problematic. Currently, about twenty-two million Americans suffer from an active substance abuse disorder. At the same time, more than one billion people worldwide regularly maintain addictions to nicotine, alcohol, or illicit drugs.

In the U.S. alone, addicts spend over twenty billion dollars per year at thousands of professional treatment centers, even though industry-wide success rates are remarkably low. In fact, the National Institute on Drug Abuse's website (nida.nih.gov) indicates that two-thirds of individuals return to drug use within weeks of entering recovery programs. At the same time, a staggering 85 percent of people relapse within a year of completing treatment.

So why are the vast majority of people treated professionally for the disease of addiction not being cured? Furthermore, if the recovery industry isn't much help, where can people find solutions to their problems?

The answers to these questions and more may lie within the framework of the disease theory itself. This conventional concept is based on the biological assumption that addicts, having been exposed to intoxicating substances, are physically unable to resist their call. Addicts are purportedly stricken from birth with this disease and helpless in the fight against its self-destructive symptoms.

While addiction has an undeniable biological component, I've learned through years of experience that long-lasting recovery is

v

much more probable when dealing with addictions from a spiritual perspective.

My only brother, Kevin, and I struggled mightily with substance abuse as young men. In doing so, we learned firsthand about the critical distinction between involuntary behaviors and habitual choices. Having grown up in church, we were familiar with the divine concept of free will and its corresponding relationship with sin. More importantly, we also knew that neither of us began to control our addictions until we learned to accept responsibility for our actions and earnestly seek godly solutions.

The reason many people still struggle with addictive behaviors is that they've put too much confidence in the science of addiction and not enough faith in God's ability to solve it. Once we recognize the true spiritual nature of addiction, we can learn by the power of the Holy Spirit to forsake our addictive entanglements and put the puzzle pieces of our lives back together.

Above all, the following pages will make the crystalline case that addiction is not a life sentence.

Introduction

The fool says in his heart, "There is no God" (Psalms 14:1).

Having experienced the wreckage of addiction firsthand, over time I began working to gain a greater understanding of the puzzling forces at play.

I started by speaking of my experiences with substance abuse to various churches and youth groups. Shortly thereafter, I was invited to join the counseling staff of the successful Misdemeanor Drug Court program in Lee County, Mississippi. I'm thankful to the judges and the many great people I've worked with over the years, as it helped expand my knowledge base and real-life experience on the front lines of the war against addictive behaviors.

After becoming an ordained minister, I started volunteering as the local Director of a faith-based group called Celebrate Recovery. This well-known program is a Christian version of the Twelve Steps to Sobriety promoted by Alcoholics Anonymous. Since its inception in 1935, the much-acclaimed AA model involves attending regular meetings with other addicts to discuss substance abuse and its related complications.

According to the organization's website (aa.org), the first of the twelve steps indicates that members need to "admit they are powerless over alcohol" and have no defense against taking the next drink. AA is undoubtedly a worthwhile organization operating with the best of intentions, but studies show that it isn't very effective in a broad sense.

While the group boasts more than two million members worldwide, many studies have found that they don't actually stay sober more often than other addicts. In fact, research indicates that only about 5 percent of AA members attend meetings regularly and maintain sobriety.

One compelling aspect of the Twelve Step AA program, however, encourages members to turn their desires and will over to a so-called "higher power." Since AA is not affiliated with a particular religion, it leaves the details as to the nature of this power remarkably undefined. Having directed many of these meetings over the years, I know this intentional ambiguity leaves the subject open to endless interpretation.

I once heard an AA member comment in a meeting that he had no real concept of his higher power. He believed that the details didn't matter. "It might as well be a doorknob," he said, as long as he could surrender his will to it. Moreover, I've seen numerous instances where the culture of this program becomes so pervasive that AA itself can become the "higher power."

In contrast, this book offers a decisively simple answer to this fundamental question. The God of the Holy Bible is the only higher power in the universe. His Son, Jesus, wishes to help you achieve freedom from your addictions, and his ability to do so is unequivocally guaranteed.

And finally, the Holy Spirit is capable of cleansing you of troubling thoughts and self-destructive behaviors in an immediate and supernatural way. The Lord loves you now more than ever. He will provide you with the strength necessary to cast aside your stubborn preoccupations with addictive substances.

If you're willing to fully surrender, you will break free from the captivity of substance abuse and enter into a fearless new life, worshiping God instead of intoxicating chemicals.

PHASE I

Discovering the Relationship Between Addiction and God

In the beginning was the Word,
and the Word was with God,
and the Word was God . . .
In him was life, and that life
was the light of man (John 1:1–3).

1

ONE

What Is Addiction?

In this world you will have trouble. But take heart! I have overcome the world (John 16:33).

Addiction is commonly viewed as a brain disease that can control the behavior and corrupt the minds of millions of addicts worldwide. The recovery industry reinforces this belief by viewing addiction as a disease characterized by a loss of control over behavior with a biological cause that is independent of choice.

Changes to the size and chemistry of the brain brought on by the habitual abuse of certain substances are believed to negatively affect certain brain functions. Alcohol and addictive drugs are considered to cause physical damage to the brain and negatively alter its ability to operate at peak efficiency.

The National Institute on Drug Abuse, a federally funded substance abuse research organization, has unequivocally stated that addiction is a brain disease beyond a reasonable doubt. Most professional treatment organizations, as well as Alcoholics Anonymous, share a similar viewpoint. While they sometimes advocate different approaches to a cure, they all promote the widely accepted model of addiction as a disease.

As we've seen, however, the vast majority of addiction recovery programs that enthusiastically embrace the disease theory have surprisingly low rates of success. Statistics show that only about one in every twenty people who enter these programs are able to both achieve and maintain sobriety. On the subject, addiction specialist Dr. Jeffrey Schaler of Johns Hopkins University wrote the following:

Addiction treatments do not work. This doesn't mean that individuals never give up their addictions after treatment. They just don't seem to do so at any higher rate than without treatment. One treatment tends to be about as effective as any other treatment, which is just about as effective as no treatment.[1]

The nature of the current disease model of addiction introduces an extremely frustrating paradox. According to this theory, addicts are presumed to have failed at recovery because of the quality of their choices. However, the very same theory clearly states that addicts suffer from a disease that actively inhibits choice. Addiction specialist Dr. William Playfair affirms this point:

> People are told they have a disease that prevents them from exercising self-control in their drinking habits, but that they must exercise self-control by totally abstaining from alcohol in order to keep from succumbing to the disease.[2]

Recently, some groundbreaking studies have uncovered evidence that cast some doubt on the validity of certain aspects of the disease theory. Certain contemporary addiction research shows addicts are not all that different from people who abstain from substance abuse. For instance, a researcher from Harvard University, Dr. Lance Dodes, who has written numerous highly acclaimed books on the subject of addiction, writes:

> Contrary to what you have heard, suffering from an addiction in itself does not make you fundamentally psychologically "sicker" or less mature than people with a wide variety of other difficulties, who generally are not so harshly judged. The feelings and conflicts that underlie addiction are easily understandable in human terms and do not set you apart from anyone else.[3]

Generally speaking, this comprehensive research makes the case that addiction is less a cause but more a symptom brought on by the necessity of dealing with the commonplace stresses of life. According to this compelling theory, addicts are simply people who need to learn how to cope with problems more effectively. He believes that many addicts habitually respond to suffering by deliberately choosing to abuse intoxicating chemicals as a means of escape. If this is the case, then choice plays a much more important role than previously theorized. Dr. Dodes continues:

> An object of addiction does not magnetically attract you—you are the one who supplies the magnetism. The good news about this, of course, is that it means you also may control the process once you understand it.[4]

If addictive behaviors are less biologically driven and more motivated by understandably mundane emotions, then perhaps traditional treatment programs should be adapted to consider a more holistic approach.

These exciting new findings then beg the following question: What role do religious beliefs play in understanding addiction? Does current research suggest any correlation between religion and sobriety? Harvard Psychiatric Clinician Dr. Gene Heyman offers the following answers:

> Religious values typically teach self-restraint and sobriety. For those who endorse religious values, this settles the issue. They do not have to weigh either the short or long-term consequences of drug use. Rather, they have to decide whether or not they are religious or whether their religious proscriptions apply to the current situation. These turn out to be simpler decisions than whether or not to have a drink. Thus, the prediction is that differences in adherence to religious values are correlated with differences in drug use.[5]

This is a monumental notion in the study of addiction theory.

Religious people are less likely to be addicts than non-religious people. Similar studies also found that adherence to traditional spiritual values and consistent church attendance were associated with lower addiction rates. Dr. Heyman continues:

> Those who prayed frequently and who endorsed the idea of a God who rewards and punishes reported lower levels of use or dependence on cigarettes and alcohol. The researchers' hunch that religion would play a role in times of stress was also confirmed. According to self-reports, stressful events typically increased smoking and drinking. But for those who strongly endorsed a belief in a spiritual world, there was no stress related increase in drug use.[6]

The value of this information cannot be overstated. Statistically speaking, religious beliefs give people a greater chance of beating or avoiding addiction altogether. This data suggests that if addicts can wrap their minds around the concepts of spiritual enlightenment, they have a much greater chance of achieving permanent freedom from their addictions.

I've been in ministry for almost twenty years, spending time during the week teaching the Bible and on weekends preaching the Word. To help support my family, I've also worked in the automotive industry for over two decades. The following illustration (one of many offered throughout this book) provides an everyday example of how addicts can view their complicated relationships with addictive behaviors.

Driving an automobile is something many of us do daily. Most often, we just climb into our vehicle and begin the driving process as a force of habit. Once we've started to move down the road, our minds tend to drift into "auto-pilot" mode, where our bodies take over the immediate process of operating the accelerator and brake pedals and keeping the car between the lines. This is how some people imagine the autonomous functioning of addictive behaviors.

Disease theory suggests physical addiction takes the wheel and controls all aspects of our abusive behaviors once we've begun using our chemical of choice. This theory asserts that the objects of our addictive desires have the intrinsic ability to control our thoughts and actions entirely, leaving us helpless to do anything other than to go along for the ride.

In reality, however, that isn't how driving works. Every driver can override this auto-pilot mechanism by swerving to miss obstacles or slamming on the brakes in the event of impending danger. This is somewhat problematic for modern disease theory because proponents believe that once an addict begins abusing their substance of choice, they cannot stop. In effect, the disease theory of addiction declares that drugs and alcohol have the intrinsic ability to turn a voluntary user into an involuntary one.

Has that been your experience? Do you believe that certain chemicals or behaviors have the power to take away your freedom to choose a different route? In simpler terms, do you drive the car, or does the car drive you?

Ultimately, we all need to understand that the vehicle of addiction does not have total and complete control over us. On the contrary, we are the ones that choose the path ahead and decide how we navigate the various obstacles in life that stand in our way.

Dr. Stanton Peele, another author and addiction specialist, summarizes his research on the subject with one profound statement. In his award-winning book entitled *The Diseasing of America*, Peele wrote, "Addiction does not mean that God in heaven decided which people are alcoholics and addicts."[7]

Think About It

1. Do you fully embrace the idea of addiction as a disease?

2. Did you know that traditional addiction treatment programs have surprisingly low success rates?

3. Did you know recent research shows a positive correlation between religious beliefs and sobriety?

Pray About It

- Ask God to help you understand the motivating factors behind your addictive behaviors.

- Pray for God to open your mind to a new way of thinking regarding attacking any self-destructive behaviors from a spiritual perspective.

- Thank God for revealing himself and his wishes throughout this book so that you may achieve a future unburdened by addictive thoughts and behaviors.

~Two~

Addiction and God

Formerly, when you did not know God, you were slaves to those who by nature are not gods. But now that you know God—or rather are known by God—how is it that you are turning back to those weak and miserable principles? Do you wish to be enslaved by them all over again? (Galatians 4:8–9)

God the Father created all of us with the ability to choose our paths and by extension our behaviors. Our Creator granted us free will so that we can live uninhibited, selfless lives that are pleasing to him. The problem is that certain people have trouble moderating their behavior in the context of this unlimited freedom. We often can't manage the privileges of behavioral self-governance, and we eventually make mistakes. To address these issues, we need to learn to better control our behaviors to avoid the pitfalls of a lifestyle of substance abuse.

One particular Scripture from Romans describes addiction in its most transparent form. The apostle Paul (whom we will discuss in later chapters) wrote the following:

For I know that good itself does not dwell in me, that is in my sinful nature. For I have the desire to do what is good, but I cannot carry it out. For I do not do the good I want to do, but the evil I do not want to do—this I keep on doing. Now if I do what I do not want to do, it is no longer I who

8

do it, but it is sin living in me that does it" (Romans 7:18–20).

Paul recognized that he was a flawed individual, and many of the behaviors in his life were built on a foundation of sin. He knew the difference between right and wrong and wished to do good things. Nevertheless, he had trouble turning his good intentions into good behavior. Sound familiar?

But before we can even think about trying to avoid sin, we must try to better understand what it is. This question has plagued humanity for years and can be easily asked but not answered. Most contemporary secular sources define *sin* as the deliberate transgression of a religious or moral law. This implies that the process of sinning breaks a law established to guide the morally accepted aspects of a person's behavior. In other words, when a person purposefully undertakes any action they know to be wrong on moral or religious grounds, they have sinned.

The biblical definition of *sin*, however, is a bit different. The Hebrew word used in the original translation of the Old Testament word for *sin* meant to step across or go beyond a set boundary. In biblical terms, committing a sin means to willingly overstep a universal line of appropriate behavior. This definition, which implies within it an understanding of what is and is not considered acceptable behavior, brings to mind the Ten Commandments.

These ancient stone tablets, given to Moses in the Old Testament book of Exodus, detailed the ten major concepts for guiding virtuous behavior in the ancient world. Generally speaking, the first four commandments deal with man's relationship with God, including guidelines for worship and obedience. The final six commandments deal with man's relationships with others, such as the commands not to commit murder, theft, or adultery.

It is no coincidence that the very first commandment offered by God involved putting him first in our lives: "You shall have no other gods before me" (Exodus 20:3). The purpose of that statement was to confirm to the people that they were to serve one—and only one—God. This was a bold proclamation because most ancient dominant cultures promoted religions that worshiped multiple gods. In fact, the ancient Egyptians maintained the belief in a complex system of more than sixty gods.

In Exodus, God continued with a second commandment:

> *You shall not make for yourself an image in the form of anything in heaven above or on the earth beneath or in the waters below. You shall not bow down to them or worship them; for I, the Lord your God, am a jealous God* (Exodus 20:4–5).

This second commandment is all about worshiping physical objects and things other than God. In biblical terms, this is known as idolatry and is undoubtedly one of the greatest sins we humans can commit.

Idolatry is all about the love of self, which is the eventual root cause of sin in all our lives. Author and longtime addiction specialist Dr. Gerald May made the crucial connection between sin and addictive behaviors in his groundbreaking book entitled *Addiction and Grace*: "Spiritually, addiction is a deep-seated form of idolatry. The objects of our addictions become our false gods."[8]

God does not require us to follow him. Instead, he invites us to do so by allowing each of us the freedom to choose our own paths. Through Scripture, he illuminates the divergent pathways of obedience and disobedience in our lives. Again, Dr. May states:

> If our choice of God is to be made with integrity, we must first have felt other attractions and chosen, painfully, not to make them our gods. True love, then, is not only born of freedom; it is also born of difficult choice.[9]

On a personal note, one of the best things about attending college in upstate New York was its proximity to one of the world's great natural wonders. While Niagara Falls is a majestic site year-round, it is stunning in wintertime. The powerful action of the waterfalls creates a cascade of water vapor that freezes at low temperatures to the surrounding trees, creating an idyllic environment unmatched in its uniqueness and beauty.

When the area begins to thaw in early spring, I've been told that it is not uncommon to see fish frozen into chunks of ice floating down the river above the Falls. Hungry seagulls will land on those hunks of ice and feed on the rapidly thawing fish. Typically, the gulls flap their powerful wings and lift off the ice just as they reach the brink of the Falls, saving themselves at the very last moment from a fatal plunge into the turbulent waters below.

However, some gulls stay in contact with the ice for too long and wait until the very last second to attempt their aerial escape. In this case, their feet sometimes freeze to the ice, and the unlucky birds cannot flap their wings fast enough to escape the deadly drop.

The risky actions of the seagulls illustrate the realities of addictive behaviors. Over the years, I've seen countless addicts spend so much time feeding their habits that they cannot let go of the substance or behavior until it is too late to save themselves.

As addicts, we must learn to deny the voracious appetites of self to subdue our addictions. We tend to bow down to the power and influence of intoxicating chemicals instead of turning control of our actions over to the Lord. Inevitably, we must learn through Scripture to balance the weight of our sins with the will of our God.

Think About It

1. How much of a role does spirituality play in your real-life struggles with addictive thoughts?

2. Have you ever used the disease theory as an excuse to continue addictive behaviors?

3. Do you believe that God can help you to gain control over your addictions?

Pray About It

• Ask God to help you understand that your addictions are little more than a deep-seated form of idolatry.

• Pray that God convicts you to commit some time and thought to the Scriptures in this study.

• Thank God that he has brought you this far in life and has the power to help you conquer any issues with substance abuse.

━ THREE ━

Sin and the Old Testament

If you do what is right, will you not be accepted? But if you do not do what is right, sin is crouching at your door: it desires to have you, but you must master it (Genesis 4:7).

As previously noted, spiritual help can be invaluable in conquering a continuous cycle of addictive cravings. Before we take a deeper dive into the spiritual nature of addiction, however, we must first examine the concepts of sin and sacrifice in the Bible.

To do so, we will begin with a brief overview of the text. Once we've established a foundation of knowledge, we can begin to understand and illustrate the benefits of a life dedicated to worshiping God instead of intoxicating chemicals.

In Genesis 1, God created the heavens and the earth. He then made all the plants and animals on the land and in the sea. He finished his work on the sixth day with the creation of humanity. On the seventh day, God looked over his creation and rested, introducing the concept of the Sabbath: "So God created man in his own image, in the image of God he created him; male and female he created them" (Genesis 1:27).

The first man, Adam, and his companion, Eve, were placed in the garden of Eden. They lived in harmony with God's creation, and all their needs were met. They were told they could eat fruit from any tree or plant in the garden except the Tree of the Knowledge of Good and Evil. If they disobeyed God's command and ate from this particular tree, they would surely die.

Amid this idyllic environment, Eve was tempted by a serpent (a symbol of the devil) to question God's instructions. The serpent refuted the claim that eating from this tree would result in death. Instead, he told her that she would become like God, knowing good and evil. When Eve saw that the fruit was pleasing to the eye, she ate it and shared it with Adam. Afterward, they were overwhelmed with fear and shame. They suddenly recognized their nakedness and tried to hide in the garden from their Creator.

God responded to their disobedience by forcing them to labor to provide for their existence. Also, these formerly immortal beings would experience death. They were banished from the garden, and God placed angels and a flaming sword to guard the entrance and further access to the Tree of Life.

This act of rebellion against God marked the emergence of sin into the world. These actions signaled the beginning of the endless human cycle of loving self over loving God. By choosing to eat the fruit, Adam and Eve put their desires above God's. This biblical story of original sin has become widely known as the fall of man.

Over the next several hundred years, the prevalence of sin in the world significantly increased. Eventually, humankind's sinful nature became so distasteful to God that he could find only a few people on the earth who continued to follow him.

The Lord saw how great man's wickedness on the earth had become and that every inclination of the thoughts of his heart was only evil all the time. The Lord was grieved that he had made man on the earth, and his heart was filled with pain (Genesis 6:5–6).

As a result, the Lord decided to cleanse the world of sin through a massive flood, choosing to preserve only a faithful man named Noah and his family. Noah dutifully obeyed God's command to build an ark to save his family and every species of animal that had been created.

As a sign of God's mercy in judgment, the earth became repopulated after the flood. Likewise, sin gained influence in the centuries that followed. People again became singularly engrossed in their lives and eventually strayed from the Lord. Because of humankind's ignorance and overall obsession with sin, God turned his attention to redeeming humanity as a whole.

To do so, the Lord revealed himself to an honorable man named Abraham, who would become the father of the Hebrew people. God made a covenant with him, promising blessings and generations of descendants in exchange for faithfulness and obedience:

> *I will establish my covenant as an everlasting covenant between me and you and your descendants after you for the generations to come, to be your God and the God of your descendants after you. The whole Land of Canaan, where you are now an alien, I will give as an everlasting possession to you and your descendants after you; and I will be their God* (Genesis 17:7–8).

The promises of God were eventually passed down through one of Abraham's sons named Isaac. He was a godly man, and the blessings of the covenant were again bestowed upon Isaac's son Jacob. His family prospered in the land of Canaan, and their numbers increased. Jacob fathered a dozen sons, who would effectively become the patriarchs of the famed twelve tribes of Israel.

The family was later forced to leave Canaan to escape a vicious famine that had befallen their land. They settled in Egypt, where food was readily available, and remained there for many years. As the Israelites increased in number, however, the Egyptians began to perceive them as a military threat.

To avoid a potential uprising, the Egyptians decided to enslave and oppress the Hebrew people. Under the authority of the Egyptian Pharaoh, the Jewish people were exploited and abused for more than four hundred years.

Eventually, God decided to intervene on their behalf. He called a man named Moses (a Hebrew who had been raised by Pharaoh's sister) to bring about the Israelite's release from slavery:

The Lord said, "I have indeed seen the misery of my people in Egypt. I have heard them crying out because of their slave drivers, and I am concerned about their suffering. So I have come down to rescue them from the hands of the Egyptians and to bring them up out of that land into a good and spacious land, a land flowing with milk and honey" (Exodus 3:7–8).

After God tormented the Egyptians with numerous plagues, the Lord's chosen people were released from bondage, and the exodus began. Moses led between two and three million Israelites out of Egypt into the Sinai Desert.

After Pharaoh granted freedom to God's people, he changed his mind and sent out an army to destroy them. As the Israelites fled Pharaoh's army, they became trapped between the approaching soldiers and the Red Sea. To preserve his people, God parted the Red Sea, allowing his people to cross safely onto dry land. After they reached safety on the other side, Pharoah's army was destroyed as walls of water collapsed and overwhelmed them.

Under Moses' leadership, the people traveled across the desert to Mt. Sinai, where God gave them the Ten Commandments. In fulfillment of his Word, God led his people to a place called Kadesh Barnea, which was on the edge of the so-called Promised Land.

Despite having witnessed the mighty power of God during their exodus from Egypt, the people were overcome with fear. They doubted their ability to conquer the land. Due to their apparent lack of faith, God banished them to wander aimlessly in the desert wilderness for forty years.

Once the generation of the unfaithful died out, the Lord chose Joshua to take his people across the Jordan River in a campaign to conquer the Promised Land. God parted the Jordan River as the Israelites carried the Ark of the Covenant (which held the original tablets of the Ten Commandments) into the land God intended for them. With divine assistance, Joshua led the people to victory over the inhabitants of that land.

Adam and Eve clearly were granted absolute freedom in the garden. However, they ultimately chose self-will over God's will by disobeying his commands. God punished them for their actions by banishing them from Eden forever.

As a result, humans are born into sin, carrying the burden of our actions as a mighty weight. In this way, sin forever emerged as a powerful force in the lives of all humankind. Therefore, we are condemned as sinners from conception and need spiritual redemption from the time we take our first breaths.

The good news is that as an addict, you are certainly not alone in your suffering. Addictive behaviors may be sinful, but they are no worse than other sins. Since all sins were inherited in Eden, all of humankind suffers under the same condition. The apostle Paul summarized it best:

> *Therefore, just as sin entered the world through one man, and death through sin, and in this way death came to all people, because all sinned—for before the law [the Ten Commandments] was given, sin was in the world* (Romans 5:12).

On some level, we all know that hallucinogenic substances are modern versions of the forbidden fruit. They are sinfully seductive in nature and offer the delusions of godlike grandeur that humankind all too often craves. When we ignore the commands of the Lord and take a bite, we are deceived into believing that this forbidden treat will transform our souls and us into gods of independence. Ultimately, a deliberate choice to abstain will result in the opposite reality—dependence on God.

Think About It

1. Why do you think Adam and Eve disobeyed God and ate the forbidden fruit?

2. Do you agree that you have free will and therefore have some control over your addictive behaviors?

3. Do you understand being labeled a "sinner" is not necessarily bad because we all fall into that category?

Pray About It

- Ask God to open your mind to a deeper understanding of Scripture.

- Pray that you will begin to comprehend the concepts of sin and sacrifice.

- Thank God for allowing you to learn about him and study his Word.

The year was 1987, and I was preparing to begin my freshman year at Syracuse University. Like many people, I was introduced to alcohol as a teenager, having dabbled with various spirits, and decided to accelerate my interest in drinking once I began to experience the unlimited freedom afforded by the collegiate lifestyle.

When I arrived at school, however, my intemperate behaviors quickly spiraled out of control into a recurring nightmare of my creation. I drank almost daily, often to the extent that I blacked out and experienced prolonged periods of lost time. I knew I was headed down a dangerous road, but I deliberately ignored the warning signs and continued my endless pursuit of intoxication without concern for myself or others.

However, I was not the only person in our family with sub-

stance abuse issues. Although my brother, Kevin, was six years younger than me, he was my best friend and a meaningful part of my life. From the moment he was born, I watched over him intently. In time we became as close as two brothers can get. When I left him behind to attend college that fall, I felt the anxiety of separation in a sharp and powerful way. But I never anticipated the events that would follow, not even in my worst nightmares.

Evidently, Kevin's substance abuse began at the tender age of 15, after I had left home for school. It started innocently enough as he began smoking marijuana with some friends. He liked it well enough but would eventually crave a more potent high. In the years that followed, he would work his way down the diabolical path from marijuana to cocaine and eventually to heroin. He would disappear for months at a time, living on the streets and fully embracing a dangerous lifestyle of abuse and depravity that would forever change his life.

Over the years, a pattern of rehabilitation, periods of non-active use, and relapse ensued. When Kevin inevitably jumped back into the perilous fray, he would do almost anything to prolong his self-destructive habit. Since his upbringing was of the highest quality, he admittedly denied that he had any reason to escape from his peaceful family life. He simply cared about getting high more than he cared about anything else.

━ FOUR ━

Sin and Sacrifice in the Bible

If we claim to be without sin, we deceive ourselves and the truth is not in us. If we confess our sins, he is faithful and just and will forgive us our sins and purify us from all unrighteousness (1 John 1:8–9).

Having conquered Canaan, Joshua and the Israelites settled in the Promised Land. For about the first four hundred years, Israel was ruled by a primitive system of regional leaders called judges. In this turbulent period, well-known figures like Samson and Samuel held the fledgling nation together.

However, rather than resting in the authority of God, the Israelites insisted on installing a monarch to rule their land. Around 1000 BCE, a man named Saul was chosen as the first king of the nation of Israel, which consisted of descendants from the twelve original tribes. His tumultuous rule was marred by dissension, and the kingdom eventually splintered.

Since Saul disobeyed the direct commands of the Lord, he was replaced by a man of God's choosing. A former shepherd boy, David, rose to fame as the youngster who engaged the Philistine warrior Goliath in solitary combat. In this story, the Israelite and Philistine armies were poised for battle on either side of the Valley of Elah.

Rather than have the armies meet in a full-scale battle, the giant Goliath challenged the Israelites to send out a single man to fight. The victor of this engagement, which was not uncommon in ancient times, would decide the outcome of the battle as a whole. However, none of the Israelite soldiers were courageous enough to answer Goliath's challenge.

Although David was merely a boy and not a soldier in Saul's army, he showed complete faith in God's power by responding to Goliath's arrogant summons and slaying him with a single smooth stone from his slingshot.

David said to the Philistine, "You come against me with sword and spear and javelin, but I come against you in the name of the Lord Almighty, the God of the armies of Israel, whom you have defied. This day the Lord will hand you over to me, and I'll strike you down and cut off your head. Today I will give the carcasses of the Philistine army to the birds of the air and the beasts of the earth, and the whole world will know that there is a God in Israel. All those gathered here will know that it is not by sword or spear that the Lord saves; for the battle is the Lord's, and he will give all of you into our hands" (1 Samuel 17:45–47).

David matured into a mighty warrior and gained favor with the people of God. He eventually reunified the twelve tribes as king and ruled justly in Israel for over forty years. As king, David wanted to honor God by building a temple in Jerusalem to house the Ark of the Covenant. But since he was a man of war, God only allowed David to design this proposed temple in Jerusalem.

Solomon, one of David's sons would accomplish the building of the temple, which symbolized the dwelling place of God. In only seven years, Solomon built God's temple in Jerusalem into one of the most exquisite buildings in antiquity. The temple, which had inner and outer courts, housed the Ark of the Covenant in an extraordinary chamber known as the Holy of Holies. Once a year, the chief priest would enter this inner sanctum to make sacrifices and pray.

The Old Testament sacrificial system (outlined by Moses in

Leviticus) was undertaken at God's temple in Jerusalem. The Israelites were required to atone for their sins by offering gifts and animal sacrifices at the temple. They would bring lambs, for instance, and present them to the priests at the temple to be sacrificed to the Lord on their behalf.

Once a year, on the Day of Atonement (Yom Kippur), the high priest would first sacrifice a bull for his personal sins. He would then present two goats at the temple door to address the corporate sins of the people.

One goat would be designated the Lord's goat and offered within the temple as a blood sacrifice. The blood of this slain goat would be sprinkled directly on the mercy seat, otherwise known as the lid of the Ark of the Covenant. The other animal, known as the Azazel goat, would be figuratively burdened with the sins of Israel and released into the wilderness, never to return. This symbolic practice, undertaken one day yearly, gave rise to the modern word *scapegoat*.

After Solomon's death, the united nation of Israel once again fractured. In 930 BCE, ten of the original twelve tribes broke away from the rest and merged to form the Northern Kingdom of Israel. The remaining tribes joined forces in the south to become the Southern Kingdom of Judah, named for its largest original tribe. This division of the tribes weakened the kingdoms and made them attractive targets for conquest by other nations.

In the years following Solomon's reign, the sin of idolatry spread like a disease in the nation of Israel. Many towns and cities built temples to worship pagan gods, leading the people astray from worshiping the one true God.

As a result of this disloyalty and sin, God allowed the nation of Assyria to conquer the Northern Kingdom of Israel in 722 BCE and scatter its inhabitants. For similar reasons, God allowed the nation of Babylon to capture and destroy the Southern Kingdom of Judah around 150 years later. The great temple and all of Jerusalem were destroyed in the process, while many of its inhabitants were taken into exile in Babylon.

During the exile, numerous prophets such as Ezekiel and Daniel began to predict the resurgence of Israel and the rebuilding of the temple in Jerusalem. In the meantime, the Persian Empire rose to prominence and defeated the Babylonians, who had previously conquered the Assyrians. Prompted by God, the Persian King Cyrus allowed the Jews to return to their homeland around 500 BCE.

Before the conquest of the Northern and Southern Kingdoms, God appointed a few specific prophets to communicate his wishes to the people. Famous men such as Isaiah and Jeremiah foretold the destruction of the temple and the nation of Israel.

During those turbulent years, the people began praying for a new leader to rise up and fulfill the role of Messiah, which means "deliverer." Because of the tumultuous nature of their history, most Jews expected God to send them a zealous, militant leader to expel the foreigners and usher in a new kingdom ordained by God.

Scripture contains about sixty different Old Testament prophecies related to the coming of the Messiah. The first of these prophecies was likely written more than 400 years before the birth of Jesus Christ. The book of Isaiah includes some of the most famous and recognizable verses of messianic prophecy. For instance, Isaiah wrote: "Therefore the Lord himself will give you a sign. The virgin will conceive and give birth to a son, and will call him Immanuel [God with us]" (Isaiah 7:14).

Isaiah continued to prophesy on the topic two chapters later:

For to us a child is born, to us a son is given, and the government will be on his shoulders. And he will be called Wonderful Counselor, Mighty God, Everlasting Father, Prince of Peace (Isaiah 9:6).

Isaiah painted the picture of a Messiah to come that would be born of a virgin mother and be the physical incarnation of God.

These two pieces of Scripture are fairly consistent with the prevailing view of the Messiah at the time of the Babylonian captivity. Isaiah's message was intended to give hope to those Jews in exile that God's holy kingdom would endure.

The following prophecy, however, is a bit of a departure from the traditional messianic interpretation and points us more toward the idea of a more pacifistic "deliverer" to come.

> *But he was pierced for our transgressions, he was crushed*
> *for our iniquities; the punishment that brought us peace was*
> *on him, and by his wounds we are healed . . . Therefore, I*
> *will give him a portion among the great, and he will divide*
> *the spoils with the strong, because he poured out his life*
> *unto death, and was outnumbered with the transgressors.*
> *For he bore the sin of many and made intercession for the*
> *transgressors* (Isaiah 53:5–12).

In these Scriptures, we are introduced to the idea of a Messiah who intercedes for us between the manifestation of our sins and God. As stated earlier, the Old Testament concept of atonement for sin involved a complicated system of gifts and animal sacrifices made regularly to atone for sinful behavior.

In these passages, Isaiah presented one of the first hints that the coming Messiah would satisfy the standard requirements of the sacrificial instrument by which all would be redeemed. These writings, completed many centuries before the birth of Christ, pointed toward a new blood covenant that would be offered for the forgiveness of sins.

Think About It

1. What kind of Messiah were the Hebrews expecting? What were they expecting him to accomplish for Israel as a whole?

2. Why did God allow foreign enemies to conquer Israel and destroy the temple in Jerusalem? Of which sin were they most guilty?

3. Why is understanding the Old Testament sacrificial system important in understanding the events described in the rest of the Bible?

Pray About It

- Ask God to help you comprehend the importance of the Old Testament prophecies about the Messiah.

- Pray that God will help you better understand the connections between the Old and New Testaments.

- Thank God for creating in you a genuine desire to read and understand his wishes and his Word.

This is a photo of Kevin and I that was taken in the Winter of 1978. At the time, my only brother was three years of age, and I was about six years older. I can still remember the excitement of meeting him for the very first time upon his return from the hospital a few days after he was born. My younger sister and I stood anxiously near the front door of our home awaiting the delivery of this tiny, precious new package. I vividly recall getting to hold him for a few moments, and then sneaking into my parents' bedroom during nap-time later in the day to watch his chest rise and fall in the rhythmic dance of sleep. Over the years, Kevin and I effectively became inseparable as we grew and matured, developing an unbreakable bond that would carry us through the many obstacles that would arise related to our eventual substance abuse issues.

PHASE II

Discovering the Relationship Between Jesus and Sin

I am the resurrection and the life.
He who believes in me will live,
even though he dies;
and whoever lives and believes in me
will never die. Do you believe this?
(John 11:25–26).

─Five─

Fundamentals of the Gospel

I am the way and the truth and the life. No one comes to the Father except through me (John 14:6).

Historically speaking, about four hundred years pass between the end of the Old Testament period and the beginning of the life of Christ. This was a turbulent time in Israeli history, marred by violent revolutions and oppressive foreign occupations. God's people finally gained independence from the Macedonian/Greek Empire in 166 BCE. This tranquil period, however, was short-lived, as the next great superpower of the ancient world came charging across their borders.

The Roman general Pompey conquered the Holy Land in 63 BCE and took control of Jerusalem. In the process, the Romans massacred priests and defiled the temple, stirring animosity among the occupied Jews for centuries to come. Despite their brutality, the Romans attempted to appease the Orthodox sensibilities of the people and avoid a rebellion by allowing the continued practice of temple worship in Jerusalem.

While their own religion was based on the belief in many different gods, the Romans recognized the importance of maintaining the traditional religious practices of the Jews. Even though they were still allowed to worship in accordance with their beliefs, the Jews longed for the coming of the promised Messiah to liberate them from the burdens of Roman authority.

The birth of this Messiah was prophesied by the angel Gabriel to a peasant woman named Mary in a small town called Nazareth. She had been pledged in marriage to a righteous man named Joseph, a direct descendant of King David. In the visitation, Mary was informed that she would conceive a child through the workings of the Holy Spirit.

Upon learning of Mary's pregnancy, Joseph decided to divorce her quietly to spare her from public disgrace. But before Joseph acted, an angel of the Lord appeared to him in a dream and told him not to be concerned about proceeding with the marriage: "What is conceived in her [Mary] is from the Holy Spirit. She will give birth to a son, and you are to give him the name Jesus, because he will save his people from their sins" (Matthew 1:20–21).

As the result of a decree from the Roman Emperor Caesar Augustus, all citizens of Palestine were ordered to return to the town of their ancestral origin to participate in a census. Therefore, Mary and Joseph traveled to Bethlehem, which was only a few miles south of Jerusalem.

Soon after their arrival, Mary gave birth to a child and named him Jesus as instructed. Christ's birth and the declaration of his arrival were heralded by angels to local shepherds in the field.

And there were shepherds living out in the fields nearby, keeping watch over their flocks at night. An angel of the Lord appeared to them, and the glory of the Lord shone around them, and they were terrified. But the angel said to them, "Do not be afraid. I bring you good news that will cause great joy for all the people. Today in the town of David a Savior has been born to you; he is the Messiah, the Lord" (Luke 2:8–11).

The name *Jesus* is an English translation of the Hebrew name *Joshua* (pronounced Ye-shu-a). It is derived from the Hebrew word that means Savior. The term *Christ* is not actually a name; it is a title. The English word *Christ* comes from the Greek word *Christos*, which means "Messiah." So Jesus Christ is actually presented more correctly as Yeshua the Messiah.

According to custom, Mary and Joseph took Jesus to the temple shortly after his birth to present him before the Lord. When they arrived, they were met by a devout Jew named Simeon. God had already revealed to Simeon that he would not die before having looked upon the Lord's Messiah. Upon seeing Jesus, Simeon said,

> *Sovereign Lord, as you have promised, you may now dismiss your servant in peace. For my eyes have seen your salvation, which you have prepared in the sight of all nations: a light for revelation to the Gentiles [non-Jews] and for glory to your people Israel* (Luke 2:29–32).

This event establishes the early divinity of Jesus, even before he was old enough to speak. Not much else is known about his childhood other than the fact that he was raised in a godly home and learned to work with his hands.

As Jesus matured into adulthood, a relative of his, known as John the Baptist, was spending a great deal of time in the Jordan Valley preaching baptism (ritual immersion) for the forgiveness of sins. John's birth had also been foretold when an angel of the Lord proclaimed that he would prepare the way for the coming of the Messiah.

Around 30 AD, Jesus traveled to the shores of the Jordan River to be baptized by his cousin John. He stepped into the waters of the Jordan and was baptized in the name of the Lord. Luke described the scene:

> *When all the people were being baptized, Jesus was baptized too. And as he was praying, heaven was opened and the Holy Spirit descended on him in bodily form like a dove. And a voice came from heaven: "You are my Son, whom I love; with you I am well pleased"* (Luke 4:21–22).

30

The voice from heaven belonged to God, identifying Jesus as the much-prophesied Messiah. John the Baptist later confirmed this notion:

And I myself did not know him, but the one who sent me to baptize with water told me, "The man on whom you see the Spirit come down and remain is he who will baptize with the Holy Spirit. I have seen and I testify that this is the Son of God" (John 1:33–34).

Having been baptized, Jesus immediately withdrew alone into the wilderness. During forty days of fasting and praying, he was tempted by the devil. Jesus rebuked Satan with Scripture three times and emerged victorious to begin spreading the gospel (which means "good news") about the kingdom of God.

When his public ministry began, Jesus met two fishermen brothers, Peter and Andrew, near the Sea of Galilee. They were the first of the original disciples to be chosen. "'Come follow me,' Jesus said, 'and I will make you fishers of men'" (Matthew 4:19).

Christ then continued to travel throughout Palestine, gaining many followers. He issued his much acclaimed Sermon on the Mount, as described in the Gospel of Matthew, to thousands of onlookers near Capernaum on the Sea of Galilee. He is portrayed in this text in comparison to Moses, standing on a hillside proclaiming the principles of righteous living through God.

While Jesus was certainly a dynamic speaker, he was also appointed by God to perform miracles. He fed five thousand followers with a handful of bread and fish, calmed a fierce storm on the Sea of Galilee, and healed countless others in the name of the Lord. These miracles established his divinity and authority to the people of the time. On the subject of miracles, Jesus stated the following: "Believe me when I say that I am in the Father and the Father is in me; or at least believe on the evidence of the works themselves" (John 14:11).

As his ministry flourished, many people began to refer to Jesus as the "Son of David" or the "Son of Man," both of which were Old Testament references to the Messiah. In fact, Jesus openly accepted this title in an encounter with a Samaritan woman.

The Samaritans and the Jews had great disdain for one another going back to the Old Testament division of the northern and southern kingdoms. The following is a portion of the conversation between this woman and Jesus regarding his role as the prophesied Messiah: "The woman said, 'I know that Messiah (called Christ) is coming. When he comes, he will explain everything to us.' Then Jesus declared, 'I, the one speaking to you—I am he'" (John 4:25–26).

So instead of avoiding the title of Messiah, Jesus settled the question by embracing it. Amid the first-century Roman occupation of Palestine, this was a perilous move. Remember, the Jews were waiting for a militant, rebellious figure to rise and end the horrors of the Roman occupation. In his public declaration as Messiah, Jesus was risking his very life. Nevertheless, he wholeheartedly embraced his position as God's divine deliverer. He stated clearly, "I and the Father are one" (John 10:30).

Jesus's initial public ministry was enthusiastically embraced by the people, but it was greeted with disdain by those in traditional positions of power. As the movement gained momentum, members of the Jewish establishment began to bristle with hatred and jealousy. They no doubt wondered, *What right does this small-town preacher have to question our authority? How dare this simple man from Nazareth proclaim his elevated status in God's kingdom?*

In the end, these powerful men would unite with like-minded others to destroy Jesus and discredit his ministry.

Think About It

1. Why is it important to believe that Jesus was born as the result of the virgin birth?

2. Why did Jesus immediately after his baptism enter the wilderness for forty days?

3. Did Jesus avoid or embrace being called the Messiah?

Pray About It

- Ask God to help you understand the importance of the real-life story of Jesus.

- Pray that God will help you to fully embrace the Gospels as spiritual history.

- Thank God for loving you enough to arrange for your salvation thousands of years before you were even born.

━Six━

Jesus Became Our Sacrifice

How much more then, will the blood of Christ, who through the eternal Spirit offered himself unblemished to God, cleanse our consciences from acts that lead to death, so that we may serve the living God (Hebrews 9:14).

If we can say with confidence that we understand who Jesus of Nazareth was, then we can begin to reconcile his position within the context of Old Testament theology. Because sin entered the world when Adam and Eve disobeyed God in Eden, humans lived under the laws of Moses for nearly two thousand years, making ritual blood sacrifices to atone for sins.

When Jesus came to earth as Messiah and gave his life on the cross, temple sacrifice became obsolete. Ultimately, this means that all of our sins have been effectively canceled by the blood offering of Christ, the aptly named Lamb of God.

The Gospels boldly proclaim that Jesus willingly sacrificed his life to offer atonement for the sins of us all. He confirmed this fact in his own words:

The reason my Father loves me is that I lay down my life— only to take it up again. No one takes it from me, but I lay it down of my own accord . . . This command I received from my Father (John 10:17–18).

Instead of continuing the ritual practice of animal sacrifices at the temple, believers need only to accept the one-time final sacrifice of Christ for the forgiveness of sins. From the beginning, Jesus understood that his life would be surrendered so that the Old Testament sacrificial system might be fulfilled in his being: "For even the Son of Man did not come to be served but to serve, and to give his life as a ransom for many" (Mark 10:45).

Having spent time with Jesus, the disciples eventually began to understand the true nature of his divinity. In fact, when Christ asked his disciples to state who they believed him to be, Peter answered without hesitation, "You are the Messiah, the Son of the living God" (Matthew 16:16).

As Jesus continued to travel and teach, he offered his disciples brief glimpses of future events. He foretold his sacrificial role and explained its importance to his followers: "The Son of Man must be delivered over to the hands of sinners, be crucified and on the third day be raised again" (Luke 24:7).

Despite everything they'd seen, the disciples stubbornly refused to believe these words. They struggled to fully comprehend the impact of the events about to unfold.

In the third and final year of his public ministry, Jesus and his disciples traveled to Jerusalem for the annual Passover celebration. This special feast was celebrated to commemorate the night before the exodus, when the angel of death "passed over" the homes of the Hebrew slaves, taking only the lives of the firstborn children of Egypt.

In the event known as Palm Sunday, Jesus arrived in Jerusalem on the back of a young donkey. The details of this event had been foretold five hundred years prior by the Old Testament prophet Zechariah. Christ's followers greeted him enthusiastically as he entered the city, laying palm leaves in his path to announce his arrival as the much-awaited Messiah.

Once inside the city, Jesus made his way to the temple. There he drove out the moneylenders and the merchants selling animals for sacrifices. Luke described the scene:

> *When Jesus entered the temple courts, he began to drive out those selling. "It is written," he said to them, "My house will be a house of prayer but you have made it a den of robbers." Every day he was teaching at the temple. But the chief priests, the teachers of the law and the leaders among the people were trying to kill him* (Luke 19:45–47).

These events raised the profile of Jesus in the minds of the Jewish elite and their Roman occupiers. They viewed him as a direct threat to their spiritual and financial control of the people's lives. They feared his emerging popularity might lead to the total collapse of institutional worship at the temple. They wanted to destroy Christ and disband his followers to preserve their power.

The Jewish high priest, Caiaphas, would stop at nothing to maintain control of his position in Jerusalem's religious and social hierarchy. In fact, he was quoted in the gospel of John as saying: "You do not realize that it is better for you that one man die for the people than that the whole nation perish" (John 11:50).

As the holy week unfolded, Jesus told his disciples to prepare the Passover meal in an upper room inside the city. At this gathering, Jesus performed the ritual known as the Eucharist or Last Supper:

> *And he took bread, gave thanks and broke it, and gave it to them, saying, "This is my body given for you; do this in remembrance of me." In the same way after the supper he took the cup, saying, "This cup is the new covenant in my blood, which is poured out for you"* (Luke 22:19–20).

Jesus deliberately chose that occasion to reveal the specific nature of the events to come. He boldly stated that one of the twelve disciples in attendance would betray him. The identity of this person was known to Christ but unknown to the remaining faithful disciples. Jesus quietly told the betrayer, Judas Iscariot, to "do quickly" what he must. Judas then withdrew from the feast to deliver Jesus into the hands of the corrupt Jewish authorities for thirty pieces of silver.

After the meal, Jesus and the remaining disciples made their way to the garden of Gethsemane on the outskirts of Jerusalem. By that time, darkness had fallen, and Jesus went off alone to pray:

> *He withdrew about a stone's throw beyond them, knelt down and prayed, "Father, if you are willing, take this cup from me; yet not my will, but yours be done." An angel from heaven appeared to him and strengthened him* (Luke 22:41–43).

Shortly after that, a large crowd of men appeared looking for the holy man from Nazareth. Judas identified Jesus among the other disciples by kissing him on the cheek. The temple guards then seized Christ, taking him to appear for judgment before a group known as the Sanhedrin. This organization, comprised of influential Jewish elders and priests, served as the religious court that guarded and interpreted Jewish laws.

The high priest interrogated Jesus at this evening's trial and accused him of blasphemy against God. The Gospel of Mark describes one particular exchange:

> *Again the high priest asked him, "Are you the Messiah, the Son of the Blessed One?"*
>
> *"I am," said Jesus. "And you will see the Son of Man sitting at the right hand of the Mighty One and coming on the clouds of heaven"* (Mark 14:61–62).

The Jewish accusers were enraged by these words and reacted swiftly, proclaiming his guilt. Christ was beaten and then taken for sentencing before the ruling Roman governor of Palestine. This man, Pontius Pilate, had developed a well-deserved reputation for cruelty across the land. However, in this case, Pilate did not find Jesus guilty of any crimes worthy of death. In fact, he tried to release him to the boisterous crowd assembled before him.

During the Passover celebration, it was customary for the Romans to release one prisoner from their jails as a gesture of goodwill to the Jews. When Pilate offered to release Christ, the crowd was incited by supporters of the Jewish elite to demand the release of another prisoner. Then those gathered emphatically called for Jesus to be executed. Pontius Pilate eventually acquiesced, sentencing him to death.

Jesus was then viciously beaten by his Roman captors. Typical Roman floggings involved delivering forty or more blows with a flagrum, a whip made of leather into which were embedded pieces of lead or bone. Although some victims did not survive these thrashings, Christ endured the vicious blows. He was taken into the palace to be prepared for execution. The guards mocked him as the so-called King of the Jews by placing a crown of thorns on his head and led him out to be crucified.

Roman crucifixion was a brutal means of torture and execution, generally reserved for criminals who had committed capital offenses. The condemned were often nailed to a cross with six-inch iron spikes through their wrists and ankles. Victims of this punishment would hang from a cross until they could not bear their body weight, thereby dying of asphyxiation.

In fact, death by crucifixion was considered so brutal that a specific word was created to describe it. The term excruciating, meaning "out of the cross," was coined to describe this inhumane ancient practice.

Jesus was nailed to the cross at around nine o'clock in the morning. He was crucified alongside two criminals on a hill outside Jerusalem called Golgotha, which means the "place of the skull." The Bible says that darkness fell on the land around noon, and the sun stopped shining. After a few hours on the cross, Jesus succumbed: "Later, knowing that everything had now been finished and so that scripture would be fulfilled . . . Jesus said, 'It is finished.' With that, he bowed his head and gave up his spirit" (John 19:28–30).

A Roman soldier pierced Jesus' side with a spear to confirm his death, bringing forth a sudden flow of blood and water. Christ's mother, Mary, and others witnessed his passing and helped to take his body down from the cross. A rich man named Joseph of Arimathea, a member of the Sanhedrin and a secret follower of Jesus, offered the tomb in which Jesus' remains were interred. To obey God's commandment of honoring the Sabbath, they had to wrap his body in a linen cloth and seal it in the tomb before sundown.

Think About It

1. Do you understand that Jesus came to offer himself as a willing sacrifice for the sins of all humanity?

2. Does the fact that Jesus felt real anguish when he prayed just before being arrested in Gethsemane make it easier to relate to him not just as God but as a man?

3. What do you think Jesus meant on the cross just before his death when he said, "It is finished"?

Pray About It

• Ask God to help you understand the immense nature of the sacrifice Jesus made for you on the cross.

• Pray that God reminds you regularly that although Christ had the power to stop his own execution, he willingly gave himself up as a "ransom for many."

• Thank God for providing you with opportunities to make changes in your future that help to bring you into further alignment with his will.

~SEVEN~

The Resurrection

The Son of Man must be delivered into the hands of sinful men, be crucified and on the third day be raised again (Luke 24:7).

On the morning of the third day, a few women returned to the tomb intending to prepare Jesus' body for permanent burial. They planned to anoint the body with spices and perfumes, following Jewish customs. When they arrived, they were astonished by what they saw. Luke described the scene:

They found the stone rolled away from the tomb, but when they entered, they did not find the body of the Lord Jesus. While they were wondering about this, suddenly two men in clothes that gleamed like lightning stood beside them. In their fright the women bowed down with their faces to the ground, but the men said to them, "Why do you look for the living among the dead? He [Jesus] is not here; he has risen!" (Luke 24:2–6)

The two men in the tomb were angels, and they announced that Jesus had been resurrected. Understandably excited, the women returned to tell the remaining disciples what they had seen. Peter and other disciples then raced to the tomb to verify these claims. Indeed, the tomb was empty, and the body of Jesus was nowhere to be found.

In the weeks following his resurrection, Jesus made about a

dozen physical appearances to his followers. One such event is described in the Gospel of John, where Jesus spoke to nearly all of his disciples a short time after his resurrection. John writes,

> *On the evening of the first day of the week, when the disciples were together, with the doors locked for fear of the Jewish leaders, Jesus came and stood among them and said, "Peace be with you!" After he said this, he showed them his hands and side. The disciples were overjoyed when they saw the Lord* (John 20:19–20).

In this instance, one of the disciples, Thomas, was absent. Upon his return, he stubbornly refused to believe that his companions had seen Christ. In fact, Thomas declared that he would not believe until he saw the resurrected Jesus with his own eyes. A few days later, Thomas was given that very opportunity:

> *A week later his disciples were in the house again, and Thomas was with them. Though the doors were locked, Jesus came and stood among them and said, "Peace be with you!" Then he said to Thomas, "Put your finger here; see my hands. Reach out your hand and put it into my side. Stop doubting and believe"* (John 20:26–27).

Seeing Jesus in his post-resurrected body with the nail and spear marks still visible, Thomas fell on his face and worshiped him. This story has given rise to the modern description of a skeptical person as a "doubting Thomas."

Jesus, being both fully human and fully God, had the absolute power to stop the process of his crucifixion and punish those who conspired to take his life. However, Scripture affirms that he gave his life freely so that you and I might have the opportunity for redemption and eternal life. Ultimately, the sacrificial offering of Jesus (who had no sin) was orchestrated by God to reverse the damage done to humankind by Adam and Eve in Eden.

So what does this mean in the context of addiction? First and foremost, we must accept that addiction is less a disease than a behavior grounded in choice. Since sins are best described as deliberate choices that cross the line of acceptable behaviors, addictions must be understood to fall into that category.

Remember, substance abuse is not worse than any of our other sins, but it is unquestionably sinful. If we lived in the time of Moses, we would be required to offer a blood sacrifice to atone for our addictions. But since Jesus did his work on the cross, our sins have effectively been canceled. Addiction specialist Dr. Gerald May wrote, "Jesus was the New Adam, the profound love gift of God entering the world to effect a reconciliation of humanity with God . . . He came for sinners who missed the mark of responding to God's love. To put it bluntly, God became incarnate to save the addicted, and that includes all of us."[10]

Think About It

1. If Jesus was aware of Judas and his intentions to betray him, why didn't he stop him?
2. What is the importance of Christ's prayer in the garden of Gethsemane?
3. Can you relate to the apostle who has come to be known as doubting Thomas?

Pray About It

- Ask God to help you understand that the crucifixion and resurrection were necessary for your personal sanctification.

- Pray that God grants you the faith necessary to avoid being labeled a doubting Thomas in spiritual terms.

- Thank God that he sent his only Son to die a horrible death so that you might have eternal life.

～EIGHT～

Jesus the Christ

For as in Adam all die, so in Christ all will be made alive
(1 Corinthians 15:22).

Having discussed the significant events that transpired in the life of Jesus, we are faced with some interesting questions. For instance, what evidence do we have that Jesus was a historical figure? How confident can we be that the accounts written in the Gospels are accurate? And finally, how can we be sure that Jesus truly was the much-prophesied Messiah?

First of all, how do we know for certain that Jesus of Nazareth lived? Interestingly, one answer to this question lies in the details concerning the authors of the Gospels. Of the four Gospels presented in the New Testament, two were written by actual eyewitnesses of the events they described.

For instance, the Gospel of Matthew was written by a former tax collector who left his job to follow Jesus. This man, also known in the Scriptures as the son of Alphaeus, is the same disciple called Matthew, described in chapter 9 of the first Gospel.

Additionally, the Gospel of John was written by another disciple. John and his brother James, known in Scripture as the sons of Zebedee, were both former fishermen called into service by Christ. So the authors of the Gospels of Matthew and John were actual eyewitnesses of the events that transpired. They wrote their accounts relying on their memories of the stories as they happened in real time.

The remaining two Gospels were written by close companions of famous disciples. The author of the Gospel of Mark was a close associate of the beloved disciple Peter. Luke, who wrote the Gospel that bears his name, was a close companion of the apostle Paul. Both Peter and Paul had personal experiences with Christ, and their combined writings account for more than 70 percent of the material in the New Testament.

In addition, corroborating third-party evidence exists for the life and impact of Christ in many written sources from antiquity. Jesus is mentioned in the Talmud, a Jewish rabbinical text that emerged around 200 AD. A Roman senator, Tacitus, also spoke of Jesus in his major writings about the reigns of such Roman Emperors as Claudius and Nero.

Another Roman writer, Pliny, included evidence about Christ in his many writings. He and his works were well-known in antiquity, as he was the governor of ancient Bithynia in what is now northern Turkey.

Finally, the well-known Jewish historian Flavius Josephus wrote the following in his first-century work, *Antiquities of the Jews*:

> Now there was about this time Jesus, a wise man, for he was a doer of wonderful works, a teacher of such men as received the truth with pleasure. He drew over to him both many of the Jews and many Gentiles. When Pilate, at the suggestion of the principle men against us, had condemned him to the cross, those who loved him did not forsake him. And the tribe of Christians so named for him are not extinct to this day.[11]

So it's quite clear that Jesus of Nazareth was an actual historical figure whose impact on his followers was significant. Nevertheless, one crucial question remains. How can we be sure, beyond the shadow of a doubt, that he was the prophesied Messiah?

As previously noted, about sixty different Messianic prophecies are included in the Old Testament. They present us with more than 250 unique details fulfilled in the person of Jesus Christ. In Luke 24:25–26, Jesus said,

> *"How foolish you are, and how slow to believe all that the prophets have spoken! Did not the Messiah have to suffer these things and then enter his glory?" And beginning with Moses and all the Prophets, he explained to them what was said in all the scriptures concerning himself.*

The disciples also witnessed many sights and miracles during their time with Jesus, but even they were slow to recognize his position as Messiah. The following Scriptures reference only a few of the Old Testament prophecies that were fulfilled in the life, death, and resurrection of Jesus:

- The Messiah would be born in Bethlehem (Micah 5:2).
- The Messiah would be born in the line of Jacob (Genesis 35:10–12).
- The Messiah would be born of the tribe of Judah (Genesis 49:10).
- The Messiah would be of the house of David (2 Samuel 7:12–16).
- The Messiah would perform many miracles (Isaiah 35:5–6).
- The Messiah would be rejected by his own people (Isaiah 8:14).
- The Messiah would come while the temple stands (Malachi 3:1).
- The Messiah would be betrayed for thirty pieces of silver (Zechariah 11:12).
- The Messiah would be resurrected from the dead (Psalms 16:10).

In a thought-provoking series, *The Case for Christ,* Lee Strobel, an investigative journalist, examined the evidence concerning Jesus. As a self-professed atheist, Strobel undertook an extensive investigation of the evidence surrounding the case for Jesus as the prophesied Messiah. In this fascinating work, Strobel uncovered the following data:

> A college professor of mathematics and astronomy named Dr. Peter Stoner wanted to determine what the odds were that any human being throughout human history could have fulfilled the messianic prophecies. In his study entitled, "Science Speaks," Stoner presented his findings, estimating that the odds of any single human being fulfilling forty-eight of these ancient prophecies would be one chance in a trillion, trillion, trillion, trillion, trillion, trillion, trillion, trillion, trillion, trillion, trillion, trillion, trillion.[12]

Strobel began his investigation as an atheist, but he completed it with an appreciation for the evidence supporting the divinity of Jesus. He concluded:

> In light of the convincing facts that I had learned during my investigation, in the face of the overwhelming avalanche of evidence in the case for Christ, the great irony was this: it would require much more faith for me to maintain my atheism than to trust in Jesus of Nazareth.[13]

Think About It

1. Did you know that two of the Gospels were written by actual disciples with firsthand knowledge of Jesus and his ministry?

2. Why does it matter that several first-century sources offer corroborating third-party evidence of the details of the life and death of Christ?

3. Of all the prophecies mentioned, which do you find the most important in validating what the Bible says about Jesus' role as the Messiah?

Pray About It

- Ask God to help you understand that Jesus has paid your debt on the cross.

- Pray that you fully comprehend the importance of the redemption process that began many thousands of years ago for the benefit of all humanity.

- Thank God that we no longer have to live under the sacrificial laws of Moses to attain forgiveness for our many sins.

Fast forward to the summer of 1993. Kevin and I were in a small church in Golden, Mississippi, listening to a sermon on the Prodigal Son. My brother had returned again from the abusive abyss, following months of active drug use to make another half-hearted attempt at sobriety. He did so periodically, whenever he ran out of money or became so fatigued by the intensity of the lifestyle that he could no longer endure it. His physical condition had deteriorated considerably, and his thought processes and memory were compromised. He was weak and alarmingly malnourished. In fact, he had not bathed in weeks, and his eyes had the vacant look of a corpse.

Whenever he stayed in my home, we had two main rules: he could not use substances of any kind and was required to attend church with me whenever the doors were opened. This particular week was special because our church was holding its semi-annual revival, meaning we attended service every night of the week for seven straight days. As we sat listening to a rousing sermon on redemption and forgiveness, the minister explained the definition of the word prodigal. This term was used in a biblical context to describe someone who wasted their talents or gifts.

This made sense to me and seemed to strike a chord in the

ever-sobering mind of my little brother. Kevin had always been a good athlete and later discovered an enviable talent for creating and performing music. He played the guitar and a few other instruments quite well and had a gift for writing songs. As we drove home after the service, we talked for a while about the message. Kevin spoke about his love of music and expressed his wish that some parts of his life had been different. After a few minutes of intense silence, he said something I'll never forget: "I can relate to the man in that story. That guy, the Prodigal Son, that's me!"

━Nine━

Jesus and Freedom

It is not the healthy who need a doctor, but the sick. I have not come to call the righteous, but sinners to repentance (Luke 5:31).

The secular definition of the word *repentance* sometimes brings to mind images of tearful admissions and heart-wrenching apologies. But the Bible's idea of what it means to repent is much simpler. While it does involve a confession of sorts, it primarily describes a process by which we transform our thoughts and actions entirely.

The New Testament was written in Greek, the Roman Empire's common language. So it is often helpful to examine the original Greek used in the Gospels for clarity in the meanings of important passages. The Greek word *metanoeo*, translated into English as *repent*, means "a complete and total change of mind." This biblical definition indicates that we must deliberately turn away from sin and turn toward God.

Jesus often taught essential principles of living within the subtle mechanisms of a parable. This term derived from the Greek word *parabole* means "to lay alongside." So a parable is a simple story that is told to illustrate a specific principle by laying alongside the actual meaning. Jesus used such narratives to explain his teachings in ways the average follower would understand. In this case, Jesus used the parable of the prodigal son to illustrate the crucial principle of repentance.

49

In this Scripture from Luke 15, Jesus spoke to a large group of people when he told the story about a prosperous man who was the father of two sons. Although it was customary for a father's estate to be divided upon his death, the younger son in this story asked for his share of the inheritance during his father's lifetime. This was a bold request because the firstborn son would have precedence in any division of a father's estate as a simple function of his birthright.

Nevertheless, Jesus explained that the father granted this unusual request and divided his property between the two sons. The younger son then set off for a distant country where he squandered his wealth on riotous living. A severe famine then overtook that country, forcing the son to hire himself out as a laborer just to survive. As a mere servant, he was humbled and made to feed pigs in the fields. According to the story, "He longed to fill his stomach with the pods that the pigs were eating, but no one gave him anything" (Luke 15:16).

At some point, the Prodigal Son's circumstances became so desperate that he longed to return to his father's household—not with the elevated status of a son, but as a humble servant:

> When he came to his senses, he said, "How many of my father's hired servants have food to spare, and here I am starving to death! I will set out and go back to my father and say to him: Father, I have sinned against heaven and against you. I am no longer worthy to be called your son; make me like one of your hired servants." So he got up and went to his father (Luke 15:17–20).

The young man abruptly left the foreign land and embarked on the journey home. As he approached the household on the road, his father saw him and was overjoyed: "But while he was still a long way off, his father saw him and was filled with compassion for him; he ran to his son, threw his arms around him and kissed him" (Luke 15:20).

The son confessed his sins, and the father received him with open arms. In fact, his return was cause for grand celebration:

The father said to his servants, "Quick! Bring the best robe and put it on him. Put a ring on his finger and sandals on his feet. Bring the fattened calf and kill it. Let's have a feast and celebrate. For this son of mine was dead and is alive again; he was lost and is found." So they began to celebrate (Luke 15:22–24).

Jesus intended for the younger son to be a character to which we could all relate. At some point, we have all dishonored God by wasting our time and energy on unruly living. We have been guilty of disgracing our Father by placing our desires and cravings above all else. We've squandered the sacred gifts we've been given, such as our talents and strengths, by choosing personal pleasure over personal responsibility.

Moreover, I cannot imagine a more classic example of wild living than a chemically fueled binge. When addicts are entangled in an endless cycle of substance abuse, we think little of the long-term consequences. We often experience the famines of life in much the same way and end up hungry and lost as we look for a way out. We frequently do shameful, humiliating things to support our habits and feed our substance-starving souls.

Fortunately, God is like the father in this story because he loves us as his children. In fact, God doesn't just love us; he is in love with us. God loves us in an all-consuming way with an eternal passion unmatched in enthusiasm and intensity. When we fail to make good choices in life, he grieves for us as any father would for a wayward child.

The hopeful message of this parable begins when the son finally comes to his senses. Luke 17:15 (KJV) says of the younger son that "he came to himself." In simple terms, Jesus said that the son recognized his sins and realized that he had become a person he no longer recognized. The son then reconsidered his position, decided to turn away from his old life, and go home. He made the humbling personal choice to abandon his innumerable sins and return to his father, which is the essence of repentance.

Similarly, we need to "come to ourselves" and evaluate our positions in life. We can continue our riotous living and suffer the consequences, or we can admit our mistakes and seek reconciliation with God the Father. On the subject, noted Christian author Francis Chan wrote:

> Some people encounter Jesus and say, "Sweet Jesus, do you want to join the party of my life with this sin, that addiction, this destructive relationship, and we'll all just coexist together?" But repentance means saying, "Sweet Jesus, you are the best thing that has ever happened to me! I want to turn from all the sin and selfishness that rules me."[14]

If we truly desire a renewed relationship with the Lord, we need to recognize our compromised states and learn to cast aside our stubborn appetites for intoxicating substances. After turning away from our addictive behaviors, we can begin the journey home to healing and wholeness.

The best news is that we never have to worry about traveling this road alone. Knowing that his son wanted to return home, the father in the parable was willing to meet him along the way. This same spiritual courtesy is offered to each of us.

When we are still a long way off, God the Father will meet us on the road with a passionate, loving embrace. We will not have to finish the journey alone because God will take each step with us and provide a scriptural road map as a guide.

Most importantly, we don't have to be clean to go back to God; we only need to commit to meet him along the way. Thankfully, God's capacity for forgiveness and compassion knows no bounds! He wants nothing more than for us to turn away from our sins and turn toward him.

While we certainly have been lost at some point, we may just as easily be found in the arms of a God who loves us unconditionally. Your road home may be littered with perils and temptations. Still, the journey to your destination will be worthwhile and rewarding. Addiction Psychologist Dr. Gerald May said it best:

> Therefore, the journey homeward does not lead toward new, more sophisticated addictions. If it is truly homeward, it leads toward liberation from addiction altogether.[15]

Think About It

1. Can you relate to the younger son and the situation described in this parable?

2. Have you ever intentionally sought a degree of separation from God, only to wish to return to his side when things went wrong?

3. Does the concept of wild living sound familiar? Have you ever "come to yourself" during a vicious cycle of substance abuse and called out to God?

Pray About It

- Ask God to reveal the importance of true repentance in fighting addictive behaviors.

- Pray that God will continually show you his love despite your affinity for wild living.

- Thank God that he is willing to meet you on the road home when you decide to repent and return to him.

─ Ten ─

The Simplicity of Salvation

Everyone who calls on the name of the Lord will be saved
(Romans 10:13).

Having established the importance of repentance as it relates to
addiction, we need to consider the next steps in the spiritual process
of salvation. Most Christians are familiar with the words expressed
in the following passage from John 3:16: "For God so loved the
world that he gave his one and only Son, that whoever believes in
him shall not perish but have eternal life."

The next verse is far less familiar but no less critical in our
understanding of God's plan: "For God did not send his Son into
the world to condemn the world, but to save the world through him"
(John 3:17).

God offered Jesus as a once-and-final sacrificial offering for the
sins of all humanity. However, this sacrifice is meaningless if we
don't actively pursue an intentional relationship with Christ. To
complete the salvation process and guarantee our positions in God's
eternal kingdom, we must fully accept Jesus Christ as our Lord and
Savior.

The apostle Paul is a perfect example of how redemption works.
First and foremost, he recognized himself as a sinner in need of salvation. Paul wrote,

Here is a trustworthy saying that deserves full acceptance:
Christ Jesus came into the world to save sinners—of whom

I am the worst. But for that very reason I was shown mercy so that in me, the worst of sinners, Christ Jesus might display this immense patience as an example for those who would believe in him and receive eternal life (1 Timothy 1:15–16).

Before his conversion, Paul was known by his Hebrew name, Saul of Tarsus. He was a Pharisee, aptly referring to himself as a "Hebrew of Hebrews," and a well-known member of the Jewish elite. But before his Christian conversion, he spent most of his time speaking out against the faith.

In fact, he enthusiastically persecuted the early followers of Jesus on a grand scale. He even assisted in stoning an early Christian martyr named Stephen, a gifted speaker and a prominent follower of Christ. As an aggressive persecutor of the fledgling Christian faith, his actions were instrumental in stunting the growth and development of the early church.

However, one day Saul of Tarsus encountered the post-resurrected Christ, which changed his life forever. He was traveling north to Damascus under orders from Jerusalem to arrest and prosecute followers of Jesus. Luke told the story:

As he neared Damascus on his journey, suddenly a light from heaven flashed around him. He fell to the ground and heard a voice say to him, "Saul, Saul, why do you persecute me?"

"Who are you Lord?" Saul asked.

"I am Jesus, whom you are persecuting," he replied. "Now get up and go into the city, and you will be told what you must do" (Acts 9:3–6).

When Saul got up from the ground, he opened his eyes but could not see. He was then led blind into the city, where he was met by Ananias, a follower of Christ.

Then Ananias went to the house and entered it. Placing his hands on Saul, he said, "Brother Saul, the Lord—Jesus, who appeared to you on the road as you were coming here—has sent me so that you may see again and be filled with the Holy Spirit." Immediately, something like scales fell from Saul's eyes, and he could see again. He got up and was baptized, and after taking some food, he regained his strength (Acts 9:17–19).

Saul then took his Roman name, Paul. He began boldly preaching in the synagogues and gathering places proclaiming Jesus as Messiah.

Paul's life is an excellent example of the patience and compassion of God. Before he came to know Jesus as Christ, Paul was one of the greatest enemies of the early Christian movement. Following the call of Jesus, he repented of his sins. He dedicated his life in service to God by spreading the message of salvation.

Not only was Paul one of the greatest missionaries ever, but he also became one of the most influential Christian writers in history. His letters account for nearly two-thirds of the content in the New Testament and have inspired countless people to find peace through Christ.

Paul outlined the basic process of achieving salvation: "If you declare with your mouth, 'Jesus is Lord,' and believe in your heart that God raised him from the dead, you will be saved" (Romans 10:9).

Remarkably, salvation is that simple. We must put Jesus first in our lives and forsake our prior entanglements with sin. This awesome gift is available to all those who choose to believe!

Now that we've established a foundation of knowledge about the principle of salvation, let us take a closer look at the concept of being born again. It can be confusing in terms of theology, but it is crucial in developing a strategy for controlling ongoing behaviors like addictions.

In the days before his crucifixion, Jesus taught and preached around the temple in Jerusalem. He spent hours instructing his followers in the faith and sparring with the Jewish authorities on subjects related to his ministry. One evening, a Pharisee named Nicodemus met secretly with Jesus to have questions regarding his teachings answered.

Jesus declared, "Very truly I tell you, no one can see the kingdom of God unless they are born again."

"How can someone be born when they are old?" Nicodemus asked. "Surely they cannot enter a second time into their mother's womb to be born!"

Jesus answered, "Very truly I tell you, no one can enter the kingdom of God unless they are born of water and the Spirit. Flesh gives birth to flesh, but the Spirit gives birth to spirit" (John 3:3–6).

The Greek translation of the term *born again* means "to be born from above." This language emphasizes the necessity of experiencing a newness of life as offered by God. In essence, Jesus was telling Nicodemus that you must let your old self die and experience a spiritual rebirth of sorts to become bound to the Lord.

This idea may have been rooted in a passage written around 600 BCE by the Old Testament prophet Ezekiel. In it, God declares,

I will give them [God's people] *an undivided heart and put a new spirit in them; I will remove from them their heart of stone and give them a heart of flesh. Then they will follow my decrees and be careful to keep my laws* (Ezekiel 11:19–20).

Here God informed the nation of Israel that despite their habitual disloyalty, he would provide them with a new heart and an improved spirit that would be more inclined toward obedience. In much the same way, God offers to remove our stubborn, addictive desires by removing our inflexible hearts of stone. Our redeemed hearts will be softened into flesh and become more flexible and open to correction. We will then be more amenable to the changes God desires in our way of life.

Jesus gives us a brand new nature when we accept him as our personal sacrifice for sin. We are born again with this new nature as we cast aside the old nature we received at birth, the one sullied by sin in the garden of Eden. Our old nature must perish at the time of our Christian conversion, and we must never allow it to be resurrected. Paul affirmed this: "For we know that our old self was crucified with him so that the body ruled by sin might be done away with, that we should no longer be slaves to sin—because anyone who has died has been set free from sin" (Romans 6:6–7).

This is where the process of repentance and salvation relates directly to our struggles with addiction. To win this battle, we must accept that our old fleshly desires can be removed with God's help. Upon achieving salvation in Christ, we experience a new birth from above with a renewed spirit that aligns more closely with God and his plan. With our newly softened hearts, we can cast aside our addictions and sinful preoccupations with intoxicating chemicals.

Again, as Christians, we are no longer held responsible for humanity's original sin. With the help of Christ, we are given a new spirit to help us to fight the battle more effectively against addictive behaviors. Again, Paul wrote, "You were taught with regard to your former way of life, to put off your old self, which is being corrupted by its deceitful desires; to be made new in the attitude of your minds; and to put on the new self, created to be like God in true righteousness and holiness" (Ephesians 4:22–24).

Addicts often have a great deal of difficulty letting go of the past. We sometimes cannot forgive ourselves for our mistakes and end up carrying the heavy weight of these burdens every day. This is why the concept of being born again has so much value. You need to put the realities of your unfortunate past behind you and learn to let go of the accompanying guilt.

Remember that the mistakes you've made qualify you to be a Christian. If you never sinned, you'd never need Jesus. You can't go back and fix your mistakes, but moving forward, you can decide not to make the same ones again. God will forgive you; now, you need to forgive yourself!

If you have not done so, I urge you to seize the opportunity to achieve salvation through Jesus Christ. You have nothing to lose except your former destructive lifestyle.

However, if you wish to continue worshiping drugs and alcohol as your gods, I suggest you not embrace the Lord's plan. Because when you are truly born again, you will undoubtedly become more interested in pleasing God than pleasing yourself.

Think About It

1. Do you fully comprehend that Jesus did not come to condemn you for your past but to save you for the sake of your future?

2. Do you recognize the eternal importance of being born again regarding dealing with your stubborn appetites for addictive substances?

3. Do you understand that salvation is the single most crucial step in your spiritual development?

Pray About It

- Ask God to allow the life of the apostle Paul to serve as a hopeful example of the redemptive powers of Christ.

- Pray that God will assist you in turning your heart of stone into a more malleable heart of flesh that will be willing and able to change.

- Thank God that he is helping you to put away your old, stubborn self to be made new in both your body and your mind.

The most significant Tuesday of Kevin's life began like any other day. The year was 2000, and he was staying with my family and me again, fresh from another disappointing attempt at rehab. He was working with us at our automotive business in Northeast Mississippi. He was always a hard worker and fit in well with the rest of our crew.

Early that afternoon, I went to the warehouse to check on something. As I headed back toward the sales area, I noticed Kevin sitting behind the desk in my office with his head buried in his hands.

The look of sadness and bewilderment in his eyes told me that something was seriously wrong. Choking back tears, he explained that one of his best friends from the streets had just been killed in a drive-by shooting in Chicago. His friend had simply been in the wrong place at the wrong time, paying for this mistake with his life. I stood in stunned silence, not really knowing what to say.

After a moment or two, I asked him what he wanted to do next. His response surprised me.

"I can't live like this anymore. That could easily have been me. I'm ready to make a change, and I'm ready to make it now!"

Although I had waited many years to hear those words, I stood in stunned silence. When I finally responded, I told Kevin we could take care of everything in a few days at church.

He responded with a profound sense of urgency, "No, you don't understand. I want to do it now!"

Within the hour, we gathered together as a family in the living room of our home. Kevin explained his wishes, and we knelt down together in prayer. He prayed in his own words, admitting his faults and asking Jesus to forgive him. He asked to be transformed that day into something different—someone totally new.

At that time and in that place, my brother Kevin Mason gave his life to the Lord. We hugged each other with tears in our eyes and celebrated together his very first moments as a Christian. It was one of the most authentic and impactful spiritual events I have ever witnessed.

~ ELEVEN ~

Final Judgment

For we must all appear before the judgment seat of Christ, so that each of us may receive what is due us for the things done while in the body, whether good or bad (2 Corinthians 5:10).

If you believe God exists and heaven and hell are real, then you should also conclude humankind will be judged at the end of this current age. This is not an abstract idea from some obscure ancient text but an actual event that will take place—whether you're ready for it or not. We will all be judged for things said and done in this life. The bad news is that our addictions and other sins will likely be a major topic of conversation.

The good news, however, is that as a Christian, Jesus has taken away our sins and nailed them to the cross. He (who committed no sin) will intercede with the Father on our behalf. He has wiped away our sins and effectively taken the eternal punishment we deserve.

Christ sacrificed himself for your personal sins and wants nothing more than for you to spend eternity at his side. But to receive this divine endorsement and enter the gates of heaven, you must make a conscious, deliberate choice to follow him.

The New Testament book of Revelation gives us a God-inspired account of the events that will come to pass in the final days. The author of this book, likely the apostle John, wrote about a vision he experienced concerning the end of the world:

And I saw the dead standing, great and small, before the throne, and books were opened. Another book was opened, which is the book of life. The dead were judged according to what they had done as recorded in the books. . . Anyone whose name was not found written in the book of life was thrown into the lake of fire (Revelation 20:12–15).

When the time comes, God won't ask whether or not you are prepared to leave this earth; he will simply make it happen. When he does, you will receive the answer to the most pressing question of all: Will your name be written in the Book of Life?

One particular story from the Gospel of Luke explains the salvation decision in its most transparent form. When Jesus was led outside the walls of Jerusalem by the Romans to be crucified, he was executed alongside two criminals. As they awaited certain death on the cross, one of these men shouted at Christ.

One of the criminals who hung there hurled insults at him: "Aren't you the Messiah? Save yourself and us!"

But the other criminal rebuked him. "Don't you fear God," he said, "since you are under the same sentence? We are punished justly, for we are getting what we deserve. But this man has done nothing wrong" (Luke 23:39–41).

Luke wrote that these two men were criminals, but we don't know what they did to earn their fates. Nevertheless, they hung helplessly alongside Jesus, awaiting the agonizing end of their earthly lives. For this text, I imagine Christ on a cross in the center, flanked by one condemned man on either side.

This scene represents the situation that all of us will face as we look death and judgment in the eye. I imagine the criminal on his left to be the one who mocked Jesus and questioned his divine calling. This man seemed resigned to his fate and exhibited no repentance or remorse.

On the other hand, the criminal on his right observed the mockery of Jesus and found it inappropriate and detestable. He defended Christ by rebuking the other criminal and asking him sternly, "Don't you fear God?" This man admitted that his behavior warranted punishment, and he was, in fact, deserving of his gruesome fate. He was right when he said that Jesus had done nothing to warrant such a dishonorable death, and he humbly recognized the divinity of Christ.

Based on this image of the criminals on the cross, one crucial question remains: Where do you stand with Jesus Christ—on his left or right side? If you hang to the left, you are not yet ready to admit your faults and accept his forgiveness. You choose purposeful disobedience and mockery over healing and deliverance. You choose substances over sobriety, yourself over God, and ultimately hell over heaven.

If you hang on the right, you've reached a turning point in your life. You recognize your sins and have repented of your self-indulgent past. You fully understand that Jesus took the punishment you deserve, and you're ready to be redeemed.

The biblical account continues after the man on his right criticized the other criminal for his lack of faith and compassion. The penitent criminal then made the following request: "Jesus, remember me when you come into your kingdom" (Luke 23:42).

The story concludes with Jesus speaking some of the sweetest words ever recorded: "Jesus answered him, 'Truly I tell you, today you will be with me in paradise'" (Luke 23:43).

This humble man only took a few seconds to ask Christ for the keys to the kingdom of heaven. Remarkably, the same can be true for you.

Remember, no fence exists between heaven and hell for you to sit on. If you foolishly choose not to decide, you have still made a choice. Like it or not, you will have taken a deliberate stance in opposition to God.

Ultimately, the consequences of not recognizing God's authority and/or deciding not to follow him are one and the same: "He will punish those who do not know God and do not obey the Gospel of our Lord Jesus. They will be punished with everlasting destruction and shut out from the presence of the Lord and from the glory of his might" (2 Thessalonians 1:8–9).

Without a doubt, you have the right to willfully refuse to follow God. But if you choose a life of independence over a life dependent on God, be prepared to face the consequences.

I urge you to make today the most important day of your life by praying a solemn, quiet prayer for salvation through Christ. If you've already done so, you have undoubtedly made the most important decision of all. Although your life will still be filled with obstacles, you will never again have to navigate them alone.

Christ spoke the following words in the Gospel of John to plainly state the marvelous opportunity that lies ahead: "Very truly I tell you, whoever hears my word and believes him who sent me has eternal life and will not be condemned but has crossed over from death to life" (John 5:24).

Think About It

1. What role does personal responsibility play in addictive behaviors? Does your behavior correspond to that of a spiritually mature person?
2. How important is your environment in determining the quality of your choices? What roles do specific people play in your recovery? Are they positive or negative?
3. Which criminal do you most resemble in terms of your attitude toward God? Knowing that you will eventually face judgment, have you decided to follow Christ?

Pray About It

- Ask God to give you the strength to take a stand by achieving eternal salvation in Jesus Christ.
- Pray that Jesus becomes your personal Savior and that you will find your name written in the Book of Life.
- Thank God for helping you to conquer your addictions so that you may serve as an example to others in the spiritual fight against addictive behaviors.

PHASE III

Discovering the Relationship Between the Holy Spirit and Addiction

For if you live according to the sinful nature, you will die; but if by the Spirit you put to death the misdeeds of the body, you will live (Romans 8:13).

~ TWELVE ~

Who Is the Holy Spirit?

Now the Lord is the Spirit, and where the Spirit of the Lord is, there is freedom (2 Corinthians 3:17).

As we study the Bible, we should begin to recognize the emphasis placed on each member of the Holy Trinity in the larger context of Scripture. For the most part, the works of God the Father are emphasized in the stories and language of the Old Testament. We learned how the universe was created and that God has loved and nurtured us throughout the history of humanity.

The works of Jesus are especially emphasized in the gospels at the beginning of the New Testament. We learned how Jesus was born, who he is, and how he gave his life to forgive sins. Although each of the gospels tells his story differently, their overall message is consistent. Jesus is God's divine deliverer, who was offered to save us all from our sinful selves.

Beginning with the book of Acts, the New Testament has been presented to primarily describe the workings of the Holy Spirit. The reality and power of the Spirit of God are emphasized in these remaining books. We will now examine this entity in greater detail to identify its practical purposes in the everyday lives of Christians.

Jesus introduced his disciples to the concept of the Holy Spirit before his crucifixion. In the gospels, Jesus referred to an Advocate or Comforter that was to come. In the original Greek, the word for *advocate* means "another that is just like the first." Christ's purposeful use of this language told his disciples that this entity would be like him. Jesus proclaimed,

And I will ask the Father, and He will give you another advocate to help you and be with you forever—the Spirit of truth. The world cannot accept him, because it neither sees him or knows him. But you know him, for he lives with you and will be in you (John 14:16–17).

Those words inform us that the Holy Spirit would not be visible but would take up residence within the hearts of believers. Christ continued:

But very truly I tell you, it is for your good that I am going away. Unless I go away, the Advocate will not come to you; but if I go, I will send him to you. When he comes, he will prove the world to be in the wrong about sin and righteousness and judgment (John 16:7–8).

In that passage, Jesus clearly stated that one of the most essential functions of the Spirit would lie in his ability to convict us of sin in our lives. Finally, Jesus said,

But when he, the Spirit of truth comes, he will guide you in all the truth. He will not speak on his own; he will only speak what he hears, and he will tell you what is yet to come. He will glorify me because it is from me that he will receive what he will make known to you (John 16:13–14).

Jesus concluded this prophetic announcement by telling us that the Spirit would be given to communicate divine truths to believers on the most fundamental levels. The Holy Spirit would come upon us like the cleansing waters of baptism and be a guaranteed gift from God for those who choose to be born again.

Jesus also offered the following instructions to his disciples after the resurrection just before he ascended to heaven:

Do not leave Jerusalem, but wait for the gift my Father promised, which you have heard me speak about. For John

baptized with water, but in a few days you will be baptized with the Holy Spirit . . . But you will receive power when the Holy Spirit comes on you; and you will be my witnesses in Jerusalem, and in all Judea and Samaria, and to the ends of the earth (Acts 1:4–5; 7–8).

The apostles (from the Greek word meaning "messengers") obeyed Jesus and stayed in Jerusalem after the ascension. They still feared the Roman and Jewish authorities, so they met secretly out of the public eye. They gathered with 120 followers in an upper room fifty days after the resurrection to pray and await direction from the Lord:

Suddenly a sound like the blowing of a violent wind came from heaven and filled the whole house where they were sitting. They saw what seemed to be tongues of fire that separated and came to rest on each of them. All of them were filled with the Holy Spirit and began to speak in other tongues as the Spirit enabled them (Acts 2:2–4).

The Bible says that many God-fearing Jews from every nation heard the sounds and gathered at the scene. They were amazed when they listened to the apostles declaring the wonders of God in many different languages. The apostle Peter then gave a rousing sermon to the assembled crowd, preaching salvation in Christ Jesus. Peter proclaimed:

Repent and be baptized, every one of you, in the name of Jesus Christ for the forgiveness of your sins. And you will receive the gift of the Holy Spirit. The promise is for you and your children and for all who are far off—for all whom the Lord our God will call (Acts 2:38–39).

The Holy Spirit rained down upon the apostles and three thousand converts that day in an event that would come to be known as Pentecost. The apostles received the gifts of healing, spoke in tongues, and went forth boldly proclaiming the power and authority of God.

The Holy Spirit is also known as the Divine Paraclete, one who walks by our side as our counselor, helper, defender, and guide. The Bible declares the following:

- The Holy Spirit is God himself (Acts 5:3–4).
- The Holy Spirit is ever-present (Psalm 139:7).
- The Holy Spirit is all-powerful (Luke 1:35).
- The Holy Spirit is all-knowing (1 Corinthians 2:10–11).
- The Holy Spirit dwells within us (1 Corinthians 6:19).

When we are born again and baptized with the presence of the Holy Spirit, we become more aware of the defects in our natural character. They are illuminated and identified as opposing our new-found commitment to conduct our lives in ways that honor God. Consequently, sins (and, by extension, addictions) become painful thorns in our sides—ones that we no longer wish to endure.

Through the power of the Holy Spirit, we recognize the need to alter our behaviors and lifestyles accordingly. This is especially true of sins like an addiction that we have previously been unable to overcome on our own. If you've so far been unable to bring your addictive behaviors under control, I urge you not to refuse spiritual help from the genuine Spirit of the living God.

Think About It

1. Were you aware that Jesus foretold the coming of the Holy Spirit before His death?
2. What is the primary function of the Holy Spirit in the lives of Christian believers?
3. Do you believe in the existence of the Holy Spirit? Have you ever had any specific encounters that support your beliefs?

Pray About It

- Ask God to open your mind to a deeper understanding of the reality and workings of the Holy Spirit.

- Pray that God will allow you to feel the powerful presence of the Spirit in your everyday life.

- Thank God for providing you the gift of the indwelling presence of the Holy Spirit in your battle against addictive behaviors.

━ THIRTEEN ━

The Power of the Holy Spirit

Like a city whose walls are broken through is a person who lacks self-control (Proverbs 25:28).

The idea of turning control over our lives to an entity like the Holy Spirit can be frightening. Having previously discussed the AA doctrine of the "higher power," we are somewhat familiar with the concept, but likely apprehensive at the prospect. Nevertheless, we should be willing to take a moment and realize the eternal value of handing the reigns of life over to the genuine Spirit of God.

If you're like many people, you've had very little success controlling your addictions on your own. You have fought this battle for years, spending so much time in secular rehabilitation and counseling that the thought of another attempt seems intolerable. I ask you now to accept the eternal salvation of Christ so that you may have immediate access to the most underrated spiritual power in the universe.

In Acts 1:8, Jesus made the following statement: "But you will receive power when the Holy Spirit comes on you." These were among the last words Christ spoke to his followers before making his final ascent into heaven. In doing so, he referenced the power that would accompany the coming of the Holy Spirit.

This English term comes from the Greek word *dynamis,* which means "miraculous might or strength." In simple terms, this word describes the ability to do things you couldn't normally do. Christ was describing the ability of the Holy Spirit to supercharge our capacity for divine obedience through choice. Paul wrote,

> *The mind of sinful man is death, but the mind controlled by the Spirit is life and peace; the sinful mind is hostile to God. It does not submit to God's law, nor can it do so. Those controlled by the sinful nature cannot please God. You, however, are controlled not by the sinful nature but by the Spirit, if the Spirit of God lives in you* (Romans 8:6–9).

The Holy Spirit can immediately and supernaturally cleanse you of immoral thoughts and behaviors. It can help you seize control of your actions so miraculously that the changes are not even difficult. The Holy Spirit, as one of his functions, was given the very key to unlocking the stubborn door of addiction! So why not place your trust in the gift that God has granted believers for that specific purpose?

When you become a Christian, the Holy Spirit will guide you like a harbor pilot guides large ships into ports of call. I know someone who does this for a living in Charleston, South Carolina. When a large vessel arrives at the mouth of the harbor, my friend rides a tugboat out and boards the ship. Once aboard, he assumes active control of the ship's helm and plots the best route to the appropriate dock or slip.

As a local pilot, my friend knows through experience where the channels are treacherous. He steers the ship away from dangerous areas. Since he's also familiar with the depths of the water, he can prevent vessels from running aground in the imperceptible shallows. His knowledge and experience are invaluable in avoiding precarious situations and ensuring that ships safely reach their intended destinations.

Similarly, the Holy Spirit will take charge of your life and steer you away from danger and self-destructive situations. It will help you avoid perilous obstacles and keep you from spiritually running aground. Most importantly, the Spirit of God will chart the most beneficial course in life to ensure a safe arrival at your final, divine destination.

Paul gave us further details on the supernatural benefits of being indwelt with the Holy Spirit. The following passage introduces the meaningful concept of the fruit of the Spirit:

> *The acts of the flesh are obvious: sexual immorality, impurity and debauchery; idolatry and witchcraft; hatred, discord, jealousy, fits of rage, selfish ambition, dissensions, factions and envy; drunkenness, orgies, and the like . . . But the fruit of the Spirit is love, joy, peace, patience, kindness, goodness, faithfulness, gentleness and self-control* (Galatians 5:19–23).

The first half of this passage describes the emotions that rule us when we are piloted by our old self, which is governed by the flesh. It references more than a few acts that may have been prominent in your addictive past, such as drunkenness and debauchery. In fact, the Greek word translated as "witchcraft" in this passage is *pharmakeia,* the root word of the modern term *pharmacy.*

The second half of the Scripture introduces us to the feelings we are likely to experience when our desires have become subservient to the will of the Holy Spirit. When our lives are piloted by the Spirit of God, we are more likely to exhibit these divine qualities in abundance. The first eight fruits of the presence of the Spirit are similar. When the Holy Spirit takes charge of your life, you'll undoubtedly be kinder and more compassionate.

The final fruit of the Spirit listed by Paul is self-control. One cannot overstate the importance of self-discipline in avoiding a vicious cycle of substance abuse. The word in the original Greek translation for self-control means "to be strong, to master or control one's thoughts and actions." Combined with the power that Jesus foretold with the coming of the Holy Spirit, we as believers have been granted all the necessary tools to take charge of our self-indulgent addictive behaviors.

In terms of addiction, the presence of the Holy Spirit has been granted to believers so that we can supercharge our ability to muster greater confidence and self-control. As someone unable to control substances on your own, the active presence of the Holy Spirit will empower you to overcome their dominance in your life. The all-powerful Spirit of God will fearlessly fight by your side as you wage your battles against addiction.

To follow the divine prescriptions of the Spirit, however, we must first learn to listen intently to its voice. As addicts, we must be primarily focused on trying to block out the everyday noises of life and actively listen for the illuminating voice of God.

Have you ever been in a loud environment, like a social gathering or sporting event, and tried to communicate with someone across the room at a distance? If you concentrate hard enough, you will find that you can isolate individual voices from dissonant clouds of sound.

Ironically, this auditory ability is known in scientific circles as the "cocktail party effect." It describes the innate ability of humans to focus their listening attention on a single voice among a bevy of background noise. This specialized listening ability has been recognized for years, although it's only partially understood from a scientific perspective.

Nevertheless, God has granted us this ability, and we can make practical use of it in terms of addiction. If you concentrate fully, you can isolate the voice of the Spirit from the cocktail party of sounds surrounding you. In doing so, you will hear the Lord's voice with clarity, regardless of the volume of any competing noise. However, learning to block out this chaotic symphony and listen carefully to the singular voice of the Spirit takes practice.

Even though we may sometimes choose to sin, the Holy Spirit will continue to guide us and will speak words of encouragement in anticipation of the opportunity to win the next battle. When we choose poorly, we are most likely suppressing or ignoring the

Spirit's commands. Since we are all flawed beings at heart, we will undoubtedly be forced to make choices outside our comfort zones to be free.

The Holy Spirit will also play a substantial role in fighting temptations and relapse. Here's how this works. When we are in a savage cyclone of substances, we often cannot remember deciding to ingest our drug of choice. We may recall the discomfort of withdrawal, but we have no recollection of consciously choosing to use the substance.

Previously, when thoughts of "using" entered our mind, we allowed the action of using to immediately follow. In other words, there was little separation between thought and action. Remember, even though the idea of using a substance may spark the mechanism of a craving, it does not have the power to necessitate an active response.

Along those lines, well-known addiction scientist Dr. Harold Urschel wrote the following:

> If you continually resist the urge to drink or use when exposed to a trigger, your body and the hippocampal system in your brain will come to understand that the trigger is not a sign of good things to come. The dopamine system will no longer be automatically activated and eventually the trigger will fail to produce a craving. That's why cravings become weaker the longer you stay sober.[16]

In other words, it is a proven fact that cravings for intoxicating substances become less powerful the longer you can resist them.

In this way, cravings are nothing more than echoes in your mind. You hear them loud and clear the first few times, but they quickly fade in volume and intensity. If, by the Spirit, you can establish authority over cravings and bring your thoughts under control, you will have developed a proven strategy to fight addictive behaviors moving forward.

Remember the story of the Hebrews' exit from Egypt found in the second book of the Bible known as Exodus? We learned that Moses and the people had been driven to the edge of the Red Sea by the Egyptian army of Pharoah. At this point, they had no apparent means of escape—only divine intervention could save them. Right before God miraculously parted the waters, Moses told the people, "The Lord will fight for you; you need only to be still" (Exodus 14:13–14).

Those words, spoken thousands of years ago, are still true today. Take the time to consider your choices and listen to the guidance of the Holy Spirit. God will fight the battle with addiction on your behalf! The Spirit of God will join you in the struggle, helping you to be victorious in the war on substance abuse.

Think About It

1. Do you believe that the Holy Spirit has the power to cleanse you of addictive behaviors?

2. Do you agree that substance abuse involves the manifestation of both a thought and an action phase?

3. How can we use the presence of the Holy Spirit to interrupt our habitual patterns and fight the battle against addictive behaviors?

Pray About It

- Ask God to grant you greater self-control as described in the fruits of the Spirit.

- Pray that God will strengthen you to separate the thoughts and actions of abusing intoxicating chemicals.

- Thank God that the Holy Spirit can serve as a wedge of choice in your fight against addiction.

━ FOURTEEN ━

The Ultimate Battle: Flesh vs. Spirit

When tempted, no one should say, "God is tempting me."
For God cannot be tempted by evil, nor does he tempt
anyone; but each one is tempted when by his own evil desire
he is dragged away and enticed (James 1:13).

God has granted us salvation through his Son, Jesus, so we may spend eternity at his side. Although the sacrifice of Christ was not justified by our sinful behavior, we may attempt to make reparations to God by bringing our lives more into alignment with his will. Remember, Jesus took the punishment that we deserve. In exchange, we Christians are expected to live in ways that exemplify the character of God.

I've always believed that people should be able to tell that you are a committed Christian without you ever having to speak a word. In fact, you should never have to tell people that you are a follower of Christ. You must prove it with attitudes and actions that make it evident and undeniable.

Assuming you have accepted Jesus and repented of your sins (including but not limited to your addictions), the question I would ask is simple: Would your life reflect Christianity's moral, ethical, and spiritual values if you never spoke a word? How different are your Saturday nights from your Sunday mornings? In other words, how much of a gap exists between how you live and how God wishes you to live?

As we've noted, the Bible indicates that the Holy Spirit lives within the hearts of believers. Along those lines, Paul wrote,

Do you not know that your bodies are temples of the Holy Spirit, who is in you, whom you have received from God? You are not your own; you were bought at a price. Therefore honor God with your bodies (1 Corinthians 6:19–20).

This Scripture boldly suggests that anyone responsible for damaging God's temple (our physical bodies) will be held accountable. Paul intended the previous passage to be a threat against self-destructive behaviors. To truly follow Christ, we must put aside our distractions, attractions, and addictions—not because we want to but because we have to.

Since our physical bodies have become the literal dwelling place of God, the Lord expects that we will honor his sacrifice by renovating our physical bodies into an acceptable residence for the Holy Spirit. Because we live in a sinful world, how can we possibly be expected to live without committing sins after we become Christians? The answer is obvious—we cannot. But we are expected to try.

Sin and obedience to God are polar opposites. Our tendency toward sin is often discussed in biblical terms as a desire to satisfy the flesh, while obedience is described as pleasing the Spirit. Our flesh is concerned chiefly with the pleasures of this world. At the same time, the Holy Spirit within us focuses our attention on the principles of righteousness. These two forces are locked in a constant tug-of-war for control over our thoughts and actions. Which one dominates your life?

Spiritually speaking, the more often you listen to and obey the voice of the Spirit of God, the less likely you will be able to hear the discord of the devil. Paul said,

So I say, walk by the Spirit, and you will not gratify the desires of the flesh. For the flesh desires what is contrary

to the Spirit, and the Spirit what is contrary to the flesh.
They are in conflict with each other, so that you are not to
do whatever you want (Galatians 5:16–17).

The word for temptation in Greek is *peirasmos,* which means "a test or trial." These complex tests do not come directly from God because he is already aware of the spiritual condition of our hearts and minds. Problems are undoubtedly placed in our paths so that we may discover our true capabilities as believers.

If you recall the discussion on Jesus' preparation to begin his public ministry, he was tempted alone for forty days in the wilderness. He rebuked the devil three consecutive times with Scripture, causing Satan to eventually depart. So, Christ himself was tempted by the devil and passed the tests with flying colors! Therefore, we may trust him to strengthen us during times of trouble.

Our daily battles with addiction and sin are nothing more than spiritual tug-of-wars. Unfortunately, our flesh presents a problem by maintaining a firm grasp on the rope. While trying to gain ownership of our souls, it will tug and pull on that rope until it comes to the realization that the Spirit within us cannot be defeated.

Paul told the church at Corinth that believers are fighting a war in their minds to control their innermost thoughts and desires:

The weapons we fight with are not the weapons of the
world. On the contrary, they have divine power to demolish
strongholds. We demolish arguments and every pretension
that sets itself up against the knowledge of God, and we take
captive every thought to make it obedient to Christ (2 Corinthians 10:4–5).

In this way, addiction is nothing more than a spiritual stronghold. We must attack this emotional fortress with all our might, taking control of our thoughts to make them obedient to Christ.

Although the circumstances in our lives may change, God's love for us never will. In spite of the nature of your current situation, the

Lord will never give you more temptation than you can handle. Paul wrote,

> *No temptation has overtaken you except what is common to mankind. And God is faithful; he will not let you be tempted beyond what you can bear. But when you are tempted, he will also provide a way out so that you can endure it* (1 Corinthians 10:13).

In this final passage, Paul wrote that we, as believers, will face daily temptations not uncommon to others. As the old saying goes, "Opportunity knocks, but temptation leans on the doorbell!" Paul stressed that God is ever faithful and will never allow us to be tempted beyond our capacity to withstand.

These are some of the most important scriptures in the New Testament relating to addictive behaviors. They encourage us to fight the battle for our souls by embracing the divine powers granted to us by the indwelling presence of the Holy Spirit. When you are in the midst of a seemingly impossible cycle of provocations, remember that God will always provide you a means of escape!

As Christians, we can entirely demolish the stubborn strongholds of our self-destructive preoccupations with addictive substances and behaviors. If we can learn to change our states of mind and redirect our thoughts in ways that promote responsible choices, we can break free from the captivity of substance abuse and experience the enduring freedom of sustained sobriety.

Think About It

1. Do you understand that, as a believer, your body is the temple of the Holy Spirit? Have you been treating it that way?
2. Do you agree with the biblical definition of the word *temptation?* Have you ever viewed a craving in the context of a test or trial?
3. Do you understand that no matter how many temptations you face, God will always offer you a means of escape?

Pray About It

- Ask God to help you "take captive" every thought related to addiction and substance abuse.

- Pray that God helps you understand you can establish authority over your persistent cravings for intoxicating chemicals.

- Thank God for offering divine assistance in the spiritual tug-of-war between the flesh and the Spirit.

The changes in my brother were evident, and not just externally. As Kevin took the necessary steps to regain control of his life, his physical appearance changed. He no longer had the vacant look of an addict. More remarkably, a major internal transformation had begun. It was a gradual process that required determination and perseverance as he reevaluated his priorities.

Eventually, he became more self-aware in recognizing the triggers (people, places, and activities) that might contribute to a relapse. His recovery was by no means perfect, but drugs no longer controlled his life. He struggled initially with cravings but could bring them into submission with the ever-present help of the Holy Spirit.

As he matured into his late twenties, Kevin started to question some of the assumptions that helped to shape the theory of addiction as a disease. Without a doubt, he made it clear to me that one of the most critical steps in his recovery involved accepting personal responsibility for his actions. "I did it to myself," he said. "I made those choices, and now I have to live with them."

Kevin entered addiction treatment for a final time in 2001. This particular facility offered a curriculum that was a perfect fit for that stage in his recovery. While in treatment, he was introduced to a beautiful young woman named Roma. They seemed made for each other from the very beginning. Once they completed treatment, they started dating while simultaneously supporting each other in their recoveries. They eventually got engaged to be married and worked together in a retail location of our family business.

Their first child, Sean Michael Mason, was born on October 4, 2002. I vividly recall my first visit with them just a few days after his birth. Holding Sean in my arms for the first time brought back memories of the first time I met my newborn baby brother. The joy of that moment will not soon be forgotten.

A few weeks later, I received a phone call from a tired yet exuberant new father. Kevin was exhausted but, at the same time, elated about the blessings of this new-found gift. We talked about how different things can be when we make choices that align more closely with the will of God.

Before he hung up, Kevin said, "These last few weeks have been the happiest times of my life!" After all he had been through, I knew what he meant.

━ FIFTEEN ━

Grace, Faith, and Deliverance

For the grace of God has appeared that offers salvation to all people. It teaches us to say "No" to ungodliness and worldly passions, and to live self-controlled, upright and godly lives in this present age (Titus 2:11–12).

Grace is the unmerited gift of God's favor in our lives. Grace cannot be bought, and it certainly cannot be earned. It is simply offered to all people as the mechanism by which humankind receives forgiveness for sins. So in biblical terms, we receive the blessings and favor of God, although we've done absolutely nothing to deserve them.

One of the most important types of grace is known as prevenient grace. The word *prevenient* comes from a Latin word that means "to come before or to anticipate." The term is used to describe the grace offered by God in our lives before we come to know him. In simple terms, prevenient grace is God's way of providing protection and direction in people's lives before they become faithful followers.

Prevenient grace is similar to the net placed underneath the high-flying trapeze artists at the circus. While onlookers are amazed at the performers' skill, the show can be breathtaking and dangerous. If the trapeze artists slip and fall, they land on the safety net unharmed and ready to climb back up and try again. We are the trapeze artists as we go through life's highs and lows, never terribly far from danger or destruction. The grace of God offered through Jesus is the net.

Faith is an essential ingredient in living a productive life in Christ. It allows us to humbly approach God and have confidence that our prayers will be heard. The writer of Hebrews offered a biblical definition of faith: "Now faith is the confidence in what we hope for and assurance about what we do not see" (Hebrews 11:1).

The Greek word used in this context for confidence means "boldness." This indicates a willingness to ask without fear or hesitation for certain gifts or favors from God. The second part of this definition offers certainty that God exists and provides for us even though we cannot physically see him.

When I think of the concept of faith, I am reminded of a particular scene in a popular movie from the 1980s. In the film *Indiana Jones and the Last Crusade,* the title character was on a quest to find the Holy Grail, which was believed to have been the cup used by Christ at the Last Supper. As the movie reaches its climax, the protagonist, Dr. Jones, is presented with a daunting test. He found himself on the edge of a large ravine that he needed to cross to enter the chamber containing the holy relic. However, attempts to do so appeared impossible to accomplish through his physical abilities alone.

He eventually decided to close his eyes and step out into the void based on the premise and the promise of faith. When he stepped into the unknown, his foot landed on solid ground in the form of an invisible bridge. It was imperceptible to the human eye but existed across the divide all along. He wasn't aware of its existence until he stepped out in faith, trusting God to solve his problem. In the movie, he then proceeded across this bridge to save the day once again.

Similarly, we sometimes are faced with seemingly insurmountable obstacles like substance abuse that we, as believers, don't know how to overcome. We look at the gap between where we are and where we want to be with the same skepticism. Since we are not physically capable of leaping the distance under our own power, we think, *How in the world can I cross that divide?*

Fortunately, God has already provided a bridge of faith to enable us to accomplish the task and avoid the fall. We simply need the courage to step onto it and believe it will support our weight.

Over the years, I've seen numerous people delivered from substance abuse through faith and the power of prayer. These divine healings are not uncommon and profoundly affect the people they bless. If you cultivate your faith, you can be delivered from your addictions immediately and miraculously.

The late Dr. Gerald May was a well-known physician and psychiatrist in the addiction industry for more than twenty-five years. He counseled many patients throughout his career and was no stranger to the concept of divine intervention. On the subject, Dr. May wrote:

> I identified a few people who seemed to have overcome serious addictions to alcohol and other drugs, and I asked them what had helped them turn their lives around so dramatically . . . They kindly acknowledged their appreciation for the professional help they had received, but they also made it clear that this help had not been the source of their healing. What had healed them was something spiritual. It had something to do with turning to God.[17]

Over decades in the field, Dr. May witnessed numerous real-world examples of what is known in the recovery industry as "spontaneous remission." He described the phenomena as follows:

> There is no physical, psychological, or social explanation for such hidden empowerments. People who have experienced them call them miraculous. In many cases, these people have struggled with their addictions for years. Then suddenly, with no warning, the power of addiction is broken.[18]

In biblical terms, this phenomenon is known as deliverance.

These life-changing events are best described as the miraculous free-dom from restraint or captivity.

Mark recorded an incident in his gospel that speaks on the subject of deliverance in an exciting way. In the story, Jesus traveled early in his ministry with his disciples near the Sea of Galilee. As he approached the shore, a large crowd began to follow him. Mark wrote,

> *And a woman was there who had been subject to bleeding for twelve years. She had suffered a great deal under the care of many doctors and had spent all she had, yet instead of getting better she grew worse* (Mark 5:25–26).

This woman likely suffered from some type of menstrual dis-order. The story continued:

> *When she heard about Jesus, she came up behind him in the crowd and touched his cloak, because she thought, "If I just touch his clothes, I will be healed." Immediately her bleed-ing stopped and she felt in her body that she was free from her suffering. At once Jesus realized that power had gone out from him. He turned around in the crowd and asked, "Who touched my clothes?" "You see the people crowding against you," the disciples answered, "and yet you can ask, 'Who touched me?'" But Jesus kept looking around to see who had done it. Then the woman, knowing what had hap-pened to her, came and fell at his feet and, trembling with fear, told him the whole truth. He said to her, "Daughter, your faith has healed you. Go in peace and be freed from your suffering"* (Mark 5:27–34).

Several important conclusions can be drawn from this story. First, we need to understand the gravity of the woman's situation. The Bible says that she suffered from chronic blood loss for twelve years. She must have had a wretched existence, but not just because of her health issues.

The Laws of Moses (presented in the Old Testament book of Leviticus) stated that no Jew was allowed to have any contact with a woman suffering from extensive blood loss. She would have been shunned by everyone around her so that they might keep from becoming ceremonially unclean.

The passage also states that the woman suffered under the care of many doctors, having spent all of her resources on false cures. Sound familiar? Over the years, I've known numerous people who shuffled in and out of addiction treatment facilities with little to no progress to show for their efforts.

Furthermore, they've likely been fed the principles of disease theory with such regularity that they feel helpless and are often unwilling to make additional attempts at rehabilitation. In addition, many families have been ruined financially by the fiscal burden of recovery programs, even though they have seen little to no improvement in their loved one's behavior.

According to Mark, the woman in question exhibited an enviable amount of faith in the restorative powers of Jesus. She felt she would be healed if she could only touch his clothes. Her faith is remarkable because Jesus hadn't yet been identified publicly as the Messiah. Nevertheless, she was aware of his teachings and likely knew about some of the miracles he had performed in the name of God.

Jesus immediately knew that someone had reached out and taken healing power. The disciples understandably did not comprehend the question when he asked who had touched him, considering the size and proximity of the crowd. Nevertheless, Jesus needed to find the woman to confirm that she had been healed and to publicly commend her faith.

When the woman realized she was well, she fell at Christ's feet and told him the whole truth. She likely told him her story, praising him for healing her body and changing her life. Have you ever taken the time to tell Jesus your whole truth?

Think About It

1. Can you relate to the definition of faith provided by the writer of Hebrews in the New Testament? Does it make sense to you personally?
2. What is your whole truth?
3. Have you known anyone in your life who has been set free in a spiritual way from addictive behaviors? Have you ever asked God to deliver you?

Pray About It

- Ask God to strengthen your faith as you prepare for the spiritual battles to come.

- Pray that God offers you a healing miracle concerning your addictive behaviors.

- Thank God for his willingness to forgive your mistakes and offer miraculous healing and sustained peace.

Kevin holding his newborn son, Sean Michael Mason. My new nephew was only a week old when I got the chance to meet him for the very first time. There were "oohs" and "aahs" to spare as we got our first looks at this precious new addition to our family. I greatly appreciate the blessing of being able to see my own children hold and interact with their tiny first cousin on a day where Kevin's life and mine effectively came full circle. Most of all, I will be forever grateful to God the Father for allowing these moments to occur and remain as enduring, blissful memories of the joys that accompany a life devoted to following and worshiping Jesus Christ.

PHASE IV

Learning To Accept God's Love and Live an Addiction-Free Life

And so we know and rely on the love God has for us. God is love. Whoever lives in love lives in God, and God in them (1 John 4:16).

─Sixteen─

Trust in God's Forgiveness

Trust in the Lord with all your heart and lean not on your own understanding; in all your ways submit to him, and he will make your paths straight (Proverbs 3:5–6).

This passage from Proverbs urges us to fully trust in God and his plan so that he can create for us a more peaceful path moving forward. Ultimately, he wants our lives to be free from any issue or obstacle that may hinder his plans for our future.

The word *trust* is generally defined as the simple reliance on the integrity, strength, and ability of a person. In basic terms, this definition suggests that trusting someone involves expecting the person to be honest, strong, and inherently capable.

By any measure, God exhibits all of these characteristics in abundance. He brought us into being and knows each of us better than we even know ourselves. He certainly has enough strength and integrity to be relied upon for help in troubled times. And finally, to say that God has our best interests in mind is a monumental understatement.

Remember, God the Father has taken away your sinful past and redeemed you through the works of his Son, Jesus. As a result, he has forgiven your sins and will work hand-in-hand with you to move forward with a fruitful life. King David said it best:

For as high as the heavens are above the earth, so great is his love for those who fear him; as far as the east is from the west, so far has he removed our transgressions from us (Psalm 103:11–12).

Not only has God forgiven us, but he has forgotten our sinful past. In his Word, the Lord promises to do so when we are born again:

This is the covenant I will make with them after that time, says the Lord. I will put my laws in their hearts, and I will write them on their minds. Then he adds: "Their sins and lawless acts I will remember no more" (Hebrews 10:16–17).

Did you have blackboards in school when you were a kid? If so, they were probably three or four feet high and stretched across most of the classroom's front wall. Teachers used these chalkboards to present class notes or solve math problems throughout the week. At the end of each day, teachers often asked a student to clean the board and prepare it for the next day's work.

When I was in school, there were primarily two ways to clean a chalkboard. One was to use a chalkboard eraser, a small soft block used to wipe away the day's work in preparation for the next day. However, all this eraser did was push the chalk dust around to obscure the lesson from the previous day. As a result, it was a terribly ineffective way of making the clutter on the chalkboard disappear.

In reality, the best way to clean the chalk off the board was to get a damp cloth and wipe it down from top to bottom. This process would make any chalkboard go from a muddled mess to looking brand new in minutes. Doing this could make the board look like it had never been used before. This is an excellent example of the sufficiency of God's grace. When you tell him the whole truth and earnestly ask for forgiveness, he effectively wipes your slate clean.

If you've ever driven a car, you know how large the windshield is on the front. It's both tall and wide and is designed primarily to protect the vehicle's occupants in the event of a crash. By design, it does so in a way that lets you see the road ahead. You're also likely familiar with the rear-view mirror, a small device attached to the windshield that allows you to monitor everything behind you. Both are important, but one is much bigger than the other.

In fact, the rear-view mirror in most vehicles is about 99 percent smaller than the windshield itself. Even though this mirror is tiny in comparison, many drivers spend inordinate amounts of time staring into it instead of focusing on the road ahead. In effect, they become distracted by the events in their past and fail to look forward to the future that lies ahead. Jesus made this point succinctly: "No one who puts his hand to the plow and looks back is fit for service in the kingdom of God" (Luke 9:62).

You cannot operate a vehicle safely if you do nothing more than stare at things in the mirror behind you. Spiritually speaking, events from your past that continually haunt you can draw your attention away from the road ahead and impede any future progress.

Finally, everyone is likely familiar with these words that Jesus spoke: "For God so loved the world that he gave his one and only Son, that whoever believes in him shall not perish but have eternal life" (John 3:16). However, few people understand the divine importance of the very next verse: "For God did not send his Son into the world to condemn the world, but to save the world through him" (John 3:17).

This often overlooked Scripture confirms that God does not condemn you for your past. He has removed your prior sins as far from you as "the east is from the west," and vows to remember them no more. So to move forward with your spiritual recovery, you must first and foremost learn to forgive yourself.

Now is the time to surrender the mistakes of your past to Christ and step into a fulfilling new life of peace and purpose. The apostle Paul said it best: "Therefore, there is now no condemnation for those who are in Christ Jesus" (Romans 8:1).

Think About It

1. Are you the kind of person that is harder on yourself than you are on others?

2. Do you believe that God can and will forgive your past mistakes?

3. Are you finally ready to accept that Jesus was sent into this world not to condemn you but to save your soul?

Pray About It

- Ask God to help you understand that he loves you abundantly despite your past mistakes.

- Pray that God offers you the strength and ability to forget your past and focus only on making the changes necessary to ensure a promising future.

- Thank God for sending his only Son, Jesus, so that you may trade away the burden of condemnation for the invaluable gift of eternal salvation.

~SEVENTEEN~

Allow God to Heal You

He heals the brokenhearted and binds up their wounds
(Psalm 147:3).

Life can be challenging at times. You, unfortunately, may be someone who has been deeply wounded by tragic events in your past that still affect you today. Perhaps you've been unable to let go of these traumas to the point where you feel they have permanently stained your soul.

If so, I have some excellent news. Christ wants to help you deal with your hurts and hangups immediately and powerfully. He knows you better than you know yourself and wants to remove your shameful regrets and drive out any remaining sadness within you. He wants to heal any spiritual scars and usher you into a new life of freedom and peace.

A story in the Gospel of John illustrates the principle of divine healing. In this passage, Jesus and his disciples traveled to Jerusalem for a Jewish festival. When they arrived, they came upon a pool called Bethesda, known to have miraculous healing powers. They found many disabled people there lying by the pool, including a man who had been an invalid for thirty-eight years.

Jesus asked this man who had been disabled for decades a question that would seem to have an obvious response: "When Jesus saw him lying there and learned that he had been in this condition for a long time, he asked him, 'Do you want to get well?'" (John 5:6) However, the man never answered the question.

Over the years, I've counseled hundreds of people with addictive issues. I've come to know many individuals through my work with the drug court system, but many more have been brought to me by concerned family members looking for hope and answers.

Initially, we sit in my office, and they begin to explain the nature of their problems. Before we get too deep in conversation, I will address the addict with a firm tone and ask the following question: "Do you want to be healed, or do you *wish* you want to be healed?"

Their answer to this abrupt question usually tells me all I need to know about whether or not they are truly ready for change. People are often reluctant to offer an honest answer, especially in the presence of a concerned loved one. They simply do not wish to upset their family members by admitting they are unwilling to alter their behaviors. While some addicts give an honest answer and genuinely seek sobriety, most will hesitate and offer the affirmative response they assume I want to hear.

If you are still struggling with addictive behaviors, answer this question yourself before moving forward. One answer I hear (more often than you might think) is that they wish they were ready to change, but in reality, they are not. In effect, they reluctantly admit that they are not yet to the point where they are prepared to accept help.

This generally means one of two things: they are either enjoying the pleasure-seeking lifestyle of substance abuse and are unwilling to give it up, or they are still holding on to some deep pain caused by a traumatic event from their past.

Along those lines, it is undeniable that many people abuse substances as a means of detaching from the problems of everyday life. Over the years, I've seen countless examples of addicts with horrific personal histories. Other people have suffered significant losses or been emotionally harmed by loved ones.

If you have ever suffered similar circumstances, these issues must be professionally addressed. However, you cannot allow these tragic events to assume a position of power in your life, serving in many ways as an excuse for habitual, self-destructive behaviors.

The first step is identifying any traumas or emotional wounds holding you back. Were you physically or sexually abused early in life? Did you suffer the loss of a loved one that still causes a deep aching in your heart? Did you do something to yourself or someone else that you think is unforgivable? If so, you need to ask God to help heal this pain so you can move forward.

Trauma is not something that we should allow to drag us down. In fact, Jesus came to lift our burdens and take away our sorrows with boundless love and compassion. Release your troubles to him, and step confidently into your future. On the subject, King David wrote: "The righteous cry out, and the Lord hears them; he delivers them from all their troubles. The Lord is close to the brokenhearted and saves those who are crushed in spirit" (Psalm 34:18–19).

Whatever is holding you back, you must learn to let it go. We've all spent too much time looking in the rearview mirror of life, and it's time to look forward toward wholeness and peace. Ask God to help you set aside bad memories of trauma and fear. Release lost loved ones into God's shelter and care. Forgive others that hurt you, and most importantly, learn to forgive yourself.

This can be a challenging process, but you don't have to do it alone. In fact, I've heard many addicts throughout the years state that they've been "going through hell" with their addictions. While I can certainly appreciate the sentiment, the single most important word in that phrase is *through*. The following well-known psalm of David illustrates this point: "Even though I walk through the valley of the shadow of death, I will fear no evil, for you are with me . . ." (Psalm 23:4).

King David understood that the Lord is always with us as we walk through the shadowy valley. We are never alone in our troubles and must learn how to travel through periods of darkness in our lives. In other words, we cannot think of our own personal hell as a destination but as an unfortunate part of our journey toward healing. Simply put, don't pitch a tent and camp out in hell! Keep moving through your personal hell until you reach the peace of Christ on the other side. Always remember that the God of the mountain is also the God of the valley.

The other answer to the question (as to whether or not you are ready to be healed) may be the most critical answer to any question you've ever been asked. Are you tired of always leaning on intoxicating substances for recreation or comfort? Are you tired of trying to drown your sorrows with a consistent flow of drugs or alcohol? Are you tired of loving substances more than you love your God?

If so, you are ready to step forward into an exciting new future of healing and hope. In the previous story of the paralytic from the Gospel of John chapter five, Jesus healed the man with words alone by simply telling him, "Get up!"

Have you moved from wishing you were ready for healing to earnestly wanting to be healed? Are you prepared to get up from your sad, stagnant state and return to being the person God knows you to be?

The Lord offers us a peace that is unlike any other. It is celestial in nature, able to transcend all fear and trepidation in an unsettling world. Jesus said, "Peace I leave with you; my peace I give you. I do not give to you as the world gives. Do not let your heart be troubled and do not be afraid" (John 14:27).

Christ will give you his peace, the kind that passes all understanding, allowing you to break free from any addictions or difficulties that may have plagued you. After all this time, are you finally ready for it?

Think About It

1. Do you want to be free from your addictions, or do you *wish* you want to be free?

2. Can you identify any traumatic events from your past that may be holding you back?

3. Have you ever truly experienced God's peace?

Pray About It

- Ask God to grant you the strength to move from wishing for healing to wanting it.

- Pray that God lifts you up when you feel your spirit has been crushed.

- Thank God for offering believers peace that can overcome our troubles and strengthen us for the phases in life that are still to come.

━ Eighteen ━

Addiction and Obedience

*As obedient children, do not conform to the evil desires you
had when you lived in ignorance. But just as he who called
you is holy, so be holy in all you do* (1 Peter 1:14–15).

As an addict, you may have been told all of your life that you've
been cursed with a chronic disease whose symptoms can be treated
but can never be fully cured. Modern disease theory suggests that addictive chemicals have the power to eliminate choice and turn you into
a helpless, hopeless slave. Having been labeled an addict for years,
you may have understandably accepted this grim diagnosis as fact.

As a result, some addicts begin to feel justified in exhibiting the
symptoms of this disease. Naturally, you may have begun to ration-
alize your self-destructive behaviors in the context of this newfound
sickness. Therefore, you might easily come to accept your fate by
thinking, *If I'm going to be treated like an addict, I may as well act
like one.* In this way, the disease theory of addiction can, at times,
be more harmful than helpful.

In reality, for many people, addiction can become a self-fulfilling
prophecy. The following passage by addiction specialist Dr.
Abraham Twerski illustrates this point:

Suppose you had an automobile that was operating well,
but a part became defective. You would replace the defective part, and the car would run well again. If, however, you
found your car was a "lemon" and each time you corrected

a problem something else went wrong, you might throw your hands up in disgust. You might justifiably conclude there is no purpose in getting the car repaired. This is what happens in addictive thinking. The profound shame that addicts feel results in their thinking that it is futile to change their ways.[19]

The bottom line is this: the more confidence you have in your ability to break a crippling cycle of addiction, the more successful you will be in doing so. As the twentieth-century American industrialist Mr. Henry Ford famously said, "Whether you think you can, or think you can't—you're right."

How many times have you said, "I am an addict" or "I am an alcoholic"? Millions of people have willingly accepted these titles over the years without fully understanding their impact in spiritual terms.

For example, Moses asked God for his name just before returning to Pharaoh to demand the release of the Hebrew slaves. "God said to Moses, 'I AM WHO I AM.' This is what you are to say to the Israelites. 'I AM' has sent me to you" (Exodus 3:14).

Responding to Moses, God called himself the great "I AM." In addition, Christ spoke these exact words seven times in the Gospel of John about the numerous titles he embraced: I am the Good Shepherd, the Bread of Life, and the way, the truth, and the life.

So, when you surrender your will to the disease of addiction by speaking the words, "I am an addict," you are unintentionally blaspheming the very name of God. The Lord doesn't make mistakes, and he didn't make one when he made you. The Bible clearly states that God created each of us in his own image and that we are effectively his masterpiece. As such, you should never give up and speak such an eternal curse over yourself and your life.

Having nearly finished this book and absorbed its content, you may have some legitimate questions about how best to translate all this theological knowledge into practical actions. In other words, you honestly believe what the Scriptures say about addiction and sin, but you don't know where to begin in terms of putting these principles into everyday practice. Consider the following illustration.

If you've ever owned an automobile that you drive regularly, you understand that it requires very specific routine maintenance. You need to pay attention to how the engine is running and ensure that the suspension and safety systems operate at peak efficiency. You need to change the oil regularly and check all the fluids to avoid unforeseen breakdowns on the journey ahead. In the real world, you take your vehicle to an auto repair shop for advice and assistance in keeping the car on the road. The shop technician then plugs the vehicle into an electronic machine that can diagnose any problems and recommend potential fixes.

In an eternal sense, I urge you to usher your body and soul as often as necessary into the very presence of God for a "spiritual tune-up." You need to plug yourself into God's company so that he can diagnose any problems and offer advice and guidance on how to keep you in the fight against addiction. Like an oil change, Christ can cleanse you by removing any harmful emotions or negative thoughts that may impede your progress in the battle against cravings.

The Holy Spirit can also heal any wounds causing self-destructive feelings or behaviors, replacing them with added measures of wisdom and peace. And finally, the Spirit will offer guidance and support to help navigate any obstacles between you and your ultimate divine destination.

Many people find that they best experience God's presence in traditional church settings or regular worship programs. Through experience, they have found that God speaks to them in these periods of worship or prayer more so than he does anywhere else.

Others, however, find it more beneficial to set aside personal time to commune with God in non-traditional settings, either in the home or other peaceful environments. These divine appointments can occur early in the morning, at regular intervals during the day, or even in your vehicle, driving back and forth to work. The location you choose matters less than the time you take to honestly speak with God and listen to his voice.

I find it best to be direct with the Father and very specific in requests for divine assistance with problems. Ask the Lord to help you fight against persistent cravings until the echoes of their call fade into silence. You can also ask Christ for help in avoiding people and/or situations that might test your resolve or challenge your faith.

The Holy Spirit will never fail to lead you down the proper path. I can offer one simple but powerful guarantee—the more time you spend in God's presence and in his Word, the less time you will spend giving in to addictive temptations. The Lord will never forsake you if you earnestly seek his guidance.

Moving forward, the key point involves replacing your corrupt old self with a new creation in Christ. The apostle Paul wrote, "You were taught with regard to your former way of life, to put off your old self, which is being corrupted by its deceitful desires; to be made new in the attitude of your minds; and to put on the new self, created to be like God in true righteousness and holiness" (Ephesians 4:22).

Ultimately, the questions become, *Who are you?* and *What do you believe?* To make better choices, you may need to make changes to your environment in order to become the person that you truly wish to be. In terms of addiction, you must ask yourself one final question: Will you obey chemicals or God?

Think About It

1. Do you use intoxicating chemicals to self-medicate, or do you simply do it for the experience?
2. Have you personally ever used your addiction as an excuse to explain self-destructive behaviors? If so, will you ever do it again?
3. Do you obey the call of chemicals, or do you follow the call of God?

Pray About It

- Ask God to help remind you that you are His masterpiece and to never again allow yourself to be labeled an addict.
- Pray that God shows you that obedience is necessary to live a blessed Christian life.
- Thank God for making you a new creature in Christ.

The phone rang just after midnight on Thursday, November 15, 2002, which is never a good sign. My mother was on the line sobbing. "Kevin's gone! Kevin's gone! Kevin's gone!"

At first, I didn't understand. Gone where? Then the reality of her words and the gravity of her tone struck me like a bolt of lightning. I was suddenly enveloped in a fog of emotional hysteria that would not soon dissipate.

Kevin, my only brother, was indeed gone from this world. Since he had not returned home from work at the usual hour, my mother drove to our store, assuming he was having car trouble. When she reached the store, she found his lifeless body inside. Kevin had been diagnosed several years earlier with a blood disorder that caused chronic problems with clots in his legs and body. One of these dangerous clots had formed and traveled to his heart, resulting in his sudden, untimely death.

I was paralyzed with grief, but I quickly recovered my senses and was determined to be strong for my family. My parents and his fiancé were understandably devastated. I drove through the night to be with them, all the while trying to gather the pieces of my shattered consciousness. I had to come to grips with the fact that I had lost my only brother, and my newborn nephew had lost his father.

The pain of that day still lingers, and the scars will remain forever. But we as a family have persevered, making that difficult journey through the spiritual valley of darkness. Since Kevin's death, our family and my faith have grown exponentially. Kevin's son, Sean, has grown into a healthy and happy young man with a familiar gleam in his eye. Although I don't see him as often as I'd like, every smile of his reminds me of his father.

To many, this may seem like a somber ending to Kevin's story, but I respectfully disagree. My brother, confidant, and my best friend may be gone from this earth, but he will always be a part of my life. "Gone where?" you might ask. The answer is obvious; he's gone to heaven! He was lost but has been found; he was dead, but his soul lives again in Christ. Without a moment's doubt, I know I'll see him again someday. And when I do, it will be just as joyous as the first time I ever saw him!

━ NINETEEN ━

The Process of Life

Therefore, my dear friends, as you have always obeyed—not only in my presence, but now much more in my absence—continue to work out your salvation with fear and trembling (Philippians 2:12).

If nothing else, the stories and teachings of the Bible make a compelling case that we as humans have been and will always be works in progress. We were born into sin due to the events that transpired in Eden and must solve this sacred problem by making a conscious choice to reject the principles of sinful living and embrace God's plan.

In theological terms, when we achieve salvation, we immediately go through the divine process of justification, whereby God moves his followers from the state of sin to the eternal state of grace. In this way, our sins are forgiven in Christ while he injects his righteousness into our hearts and minds. The good news is that this justification process is accomplished entirely by God and requires no effort on our part to complete. Paul said, "Therefore, if anyone is in Christ, he is a new creation; the old has gone, the new has come!" (2 Corinthians 5:17)

The bad news is that from this point forward, we are held responsible for working out our salvation by bringing our lives into further alignment with God's will. Having been justified by Christ, we must begin the lifelong process of learning to live in ways that are pleasing to God. In biblical terms, this is a process known as sanctification. Paul described it this way:

May God himself, the God of peace, sanctify you through and through. May your whole spirit, soul and body be kept blameless at the coming of our Lord Jesus Christ (1 Thessalonians 5:23).

This term comes from the Latin word *sanctus*, which means "to be set apart or to be made holy." In practice, it's how God helps believers live out their lives in ways that mirror Christ. Sanctification is an ongoing process that God has ordained to assist Christians with the work of becoming purified in both thoughts and actions through the divine mechanism of grace.

Because we were born into sin, we can never expect to achieve full sanctification in our temporal lives. However, we are encouraged to keep pressing towards the mark by avoiding sinful thoughts and behaviors when possible. Having made the crucial case that addiction is a deep-seated form of idolatry, our addictive behaviors fall into the general category of sin and must be dealt with accordingly.

Here is the best news of all. Even though we as Christians can never fully complete the sanctification process in our earthly lives and earn total freedom from sin, we can expect to become entirely free from the diabolical grip of addictive behaviors. Not surprisingly, the very best way to try to accomplish this task is to do so at Christ's side:

Come to me, all you who are weary and burdened, and I will give you rest. Take my yoke upon you and learn from me, for I am gentle and humble in heart, and you will find rest for your souls (Matthew 11:28–29).

Jesus spoke these words in the Gospel of Matthew using imagery that the average listener in first-century Judea would understand. He described a yoke, a wooden device used to attach two oxen to a cart or plow. A typical yoke had a rounded collar that went around the neck of each animal to ensure a solid connection between them and the object to be pulled.

Of the two oxen that shared the yoke, the first was an older, stronger, and more experienced animal. Since the second ox was generally younger, it lacked the strength and experience to bear the plow's weight alone. Consequently, the older animal carried the majority of the load and chose the path ahead, while the younger beast followed alongside and learned.

This is what Christ wishes for us to do. He is willing to help us bear our burdens and lighten our load while teaching us how to move forward in life following a divinely chosen path. In doing so, Jesus offers us rest in both the temporal and eternal settings.

Remember, Jesus Christ was the only person ever to live an entire life without sin. In reality, we can never replicate the virtuous life of Jesus, but we are certainly expected to try. When we inevitably fall short in this task, we need to show remorse for our sinful actions and ask the Father for forgiveness. However, we cannot expect to make significant progress towards reaching the end goal of sanctification without being yoked to Christ.

Numerous studies have indicated that most addicts began using and/or abusing substances in social groups. In fact, my brother and I initially experimented with intoxicating substances within small groups of friends. If this was the case for you as well, do you honestly believe that you can remain in that same environment and have any chance at all of changing your behavior?

Not surprisingly, most addicts are often hesitant to make even temporary changes to their addictive environments. Substance abusers, like most people, are comfortable in familiar places and around familiar faces. Comfort, however, can be deceiving because it can mask the destructive realities of unhealthy situations. If your environment has contributed to your addiction, it must change for it to contribute to your sobriety.

Paul addressed this in his second letter to the church at Corinth: "Do not be yoked together with unbelievers. For what do righteousness and wickedness have in common? Or what fellowship can light have with the darkness?" (2 Corinthians 6:14).

Remember, you are not a bad person in God's eyes, simply a person who has done bad things. As an addict, you may have spent years chasing a persistent state of intoxication, but you've likely not done so alone. The people you surround yourself with may be the single most critical factor in helping or hurting your recovery. And since the Bible clearly states that bad company corrupts good character, you must constantly evaluate whether or not the people around you have your best interests in mind. The bottom line is this: choose very carefully the people you become yoked to in your recovery process.

Finally, consequences alone rarely persuade people to discontinue addictive behaviors. So the notion that people can wait until they hit "rock bottom" in their recovery is not only absurd but dangerous. This idea often encourages addicts to continue using drugs and/or alcohol until they feel they've reached this metaphorical bottom.

However, since most addicts only recognize their personal bottom in retrospect, this concept encourages the continuation of self-destructive behaviors until an emotional or physical decline prevails. Realistically, when you've reached the point where using chemicals is more valuable to you than sobriety and life itself, you've hit rock bottom! All addicts make regrettable choices that result in unfortunate consequences. In simpler terms, you've reached rock bottom when you make a final, permanent choice to stop digging.

Think About It

1. Do you think you see yourself the way God sees you?

2. Have you ever used the "rock bottom" principle as an excuse to continue addictive behaviors?

3. Does your current environment either help or hurt your prospects for sustained sobriety?

Pray About It

- Ask God to offer you daily assistance in your personal process of sanctification.

- Pray that God shows you how to enter into his presence so that you may be effectively yoked to Christ.

- Thank God for loving you throughout this process and offering you the hope of a future free of addictive entanglements.

ᐸ TWENTY ᐳ

Now Go Forth

*"Therefore go and make disciples of all nations, baptizing
them in the name of the Father and of the Son and of the
Holy Spirit, and teaching them to obey everything I have
commanded you. And surely I am with you always, to the
very end of the age"* (Matthew 28:19–20).

Christ made about a dozen appearances to various people in his
post-resurrection body. The final and most important of these was
on a mountaintop in Galilee, where Jesus had instructed his followers to gather. Eleven of the original twelve disciples were present
when Jesus spoke the above words on the critical subject of discipleship. In spiritual terms, this idea generally describes the process by
which believers help others to learn to be like Christ.

Along these lines, a simple story in the Gospel of Matthew
offers us a quick glimpse into how Christ went about gaining disciples:

*As Jesus was walking beside the Sea of Galilee, he saw two
brothers, Simon called Peter and his brother Andrew. They
were casting a net into the lake, for they were fisherman.
"Come follow me," Jesus said, "and I will send you out to
fish for people." At once, they left their nets and followed him*
(Matthew 4:18–20).

In this passage, Jesus happens upon two brothers named Peter
and Andrew in Capernaum on the shores of the Sea of Galilee. They

were fishermen who were undoubtedly in the middle of what was shaping up to be an unproductive day. When he called out to them, he spoke in simple terms that he knew they would understand. In effect, he took something they were very familiar with, their profession, and made it new for them by drawing them away from their old lives and into ministry at his side.

In this way, Jesus chose Peter and Andrew as his first disciples by calling them into service to use the everyday skills they'd learned over the years as fishermen. If you've ever spent any time fishing, you no doubt understand that it requires a great deal of attention and inordinate amounts of patience. It just so happens that these very same skills are necessary for making Christian disciples.

In much the same way, as a former addict, you are uniquely qualified to speak God's truth to others who've likewise struggled. You've fought your way through the gauntlet of addiction. You are aware of the many obstacles facing people genuinely searching for answers. Perhaps, God has brought you through these challenges so that you may be of encouragement to others who have suffered in similar ways.

Your individual struggles may have been painful, but they uniquely qualify you to share your trials and triumphs with others. In fact, you have something that many people in the secular recovery industry do not have—credibility with people who struggle with addictive behaviors. You can offer sympathy and empathy to those looking for a beacon of hope in a dark, dismal land. Your experiences, both good and bad, could help change someone's life.

The Bible affirms that we should use our experiences and divine giftings to help others understand how much God loves them and wishes them to be free: "Each one should use whatever gift he has received to serve others, faithfully administering God's grace in its various forms" (1 Peter 4:10).

Eventually, you may come to view the struggles in your past as a gift of sorts, preparing the way for you to emerge victorious from this existential struggle and provide guidance to others facing similar circumstances.

If God has done a mighty work in you, then you should try to pay it forward by telling others that he wishes to offer them a similarly miraculous opportunity. Paul expressed a parallel sentiment in which he recognized the eternal value inherent in the mistakes and struggles that he faced in his checkered past: "Now I want you to know, brothers, that what has happened to me has really served to advance the gospel" (Philippians 1:12).

You're probably familiar with the old idiom that says, "You can lead a horse to water, but you can't make him drink." This metaphorical saying dates back to a sixteenth-century English writer named John Heywood. It means that while you can lead others to a place or activity that is in their best interests, you cannot require them to avail themselves of the opportunities for growth that await.

The ministry of discipleship often works similarly. As believers, we have experienced the tremendous benefits and peace that come with an eternal relationship with God the Father through Jesus Christ. And while we Christians truly understand the infinite value of this relationship, we cannot force others to make a salvation decision that would no doubt change their lives.

As disciples, however, we must not get discouraged in this mission when others delay their decisions or refuse to follow God. We can only show love to those we encounter and support them along the way. Ultimately, we cannot require them to drink the living water of Christ. But we can absolutely accomplish the true goal of discipleship, which is to make them thirsty for it.

Having completed this study, you should now be equipped to step out of your shell and join God in the spiritual fight for the souls of the lost. Remember, your "old self" is dead, and the "new self" has taken control of your thoughts and actions.

Take full advantage of this gift by living a life dedicated to expanding the kingdom of God. Use what you've learned and the gifts you've been given and help make disciples of others. Spread the good news of the Gospel of Christ and live the rest of your life worshiping God instead of intoxicating chemicals!

Think About It

1. In what ways have you changed since you began this study?

2. Have you ever thought about helping others with similar addictive issues?

3. Are you ready to take what you've learned and help others develop a genuine thirst for God?

Pray About It

- Ask God to speak truth into your life as you prepare to begin your personal discipleship process.

- Pray that God gives you the words to say when allowed to speak with others about the benefits of developing a personal relationship with Christ.

- Thank God for offering you everlasting grace as you plot a course toward a future life of blessings and sobriety in Jesus' name.

NOTES

[1] Jeffrey A.Schaler, *Addiction Is a Choice* (Peru, IL: Carus Publishing Company, 2000) p.44.

[2] William L. Playfair, *The Useful Lie* (Wheaton, IL: Crossway Books, 1991) p.58.

[3] Lance Dodes, MD, *The Heart of Addiction* (New York, NY: Harpercollins Publishers, 2002) p.22.

[4] ibid, p.119.

[5] Gene M. Heyman, *Addiction: A Disorder of Choice* (Cambridge, MA: Harvard University Press, 2009) p.166.

[6] ibid, p.164

[7] Stanton Peele, *Diseasing of America* (San Francisco, CA: Jossey-Bass Publishers, 1995) p.3.

[8] Gerald G. May, *Addiction & Grace* (New York, NY: HarperCollins Publishers, 1988) p.13.

[9] ibid, p.94.

[10] ibid, p.115.

[11] Flavius Josephus, *Antiquities of the Jews* Text from Book 18: Chapter 3, p.3.

[12] Lee Strobel, *The Case for Christ* (Grand Rapids, MI: Zondervan, 1998) p.183.

[13] ibid, p.265.

[14] Francis Chan, *Forgotten God* (Colorado Springs, CO: David C. Cooke, 2009) p.124.

[15] May, p.98.

[16] Harold C. Urschell, III, MD, *Healing the Addicted Brain* (Naperville, IL: Sourcebooks, Inc, 2009) p.60.

[17] May, p.6–7.

[18] ibid, p.153.

[19] Abraham J. Twerski, MD, *Addictive Thinking* (Center City, MN: Hazelden, 1990) p.69.

About the Author

MICHAEL K. MASON is a writer, counselor, and ordained minister from Tupelo, MS. He holds a bachelors degree from Syracuse University and served for years on the staff of the successful misdemeanor drug court program in Lee County, Mississippi.

He is the author of two additional books: *Addiction and God—Reconciling Science with the Spirit,* and the *Amazing Grace Addiction Bible Study.* He also serves as the host of a weekly radio program called *Addiction and Grace* that airs on the Kingdom Broadcasting Network in Mississippi.

Printed in the USA
CPSIA information can be obtained
at www.ICGtesting.com
LVHW011256270324
775527LV00013B/849